Keith Waterhouse, born in 1929, is the son of a Leeds costermonger. He worked in a cobbler's shop, an undertaker's and a garage before launching into journalism and becoming a writer. *Mrs Pooter's Diary* is his ninth novel. His first, published in 1956, was *There is a Happy Land*. This was followed by the brilliantly successful *Billy Liar* in 1960, which was filmed, televised and turned into a stage play; *Jubb* (1963), *The Bucket Shop* (1968), *Billy Liar on the Moon* (1975), *Office Life* (1978), *Maggie Muggins* (1981) and *In the Mood* (1983).

Keith Waterhouse has written extensively for the theatre, cinema and television. He is a frequent contributor to *Punch* and since 1970, has had his own column in the *Daily Mirror*. The first selection of his pieces from *Punch, The Passing of the Third-Floor Buck*, was published in 1974 and a second, *Fanny Peculiar* in 1983. Selections of his *Daily Mirror* pieces, *Mondays, Thursdays* and *Rhubarb, Rhubarb and Other Noises*, appeared in 1976 and 1979.

Author photograph by Fay Godwin

Also by Keith Waterhouse

IN THE MOOD

and published by Black Swan

Mrs Pooter's Diary

Keith Waterhouse

BLACK SWAN

MRS POOTER'S DIARY

A BLACK SWAN BOOK 0 552 99117 1

Originally published in Great Britain by
Michael Joseph Ltd.

PRINTING HISTORY
Michael Joseph edition published 1983
Black Swan edition published 1984
Black Swan edition reprinted 1985

Copyright © Keith Waterhouse Ltd. 1983

This book is set in 11/12 Mallard

Black Swan Books are published by
Transworld Publishers Ltd.,
Century House, 61-63 Uxbridge Road,
Ealing, London W5 5SA

Made and printed in Great Britain by the
Guernsey Press Co. Ltd., Guernsey, Channel Islands.

To the memory of
GEORGE AND WEEDON GROSSMITH

Contents

Introduction

Sir, May I crave the courtesy of your columns to put paid to a foul canard – namely, that I have had the temerity to re-write *The Diary of a Nobody*.

Sir, I have not – would not – dare not! What I have ventured to do is to add the merest footnote to that major classic of English humour (always, for some odd reason, dubbed a *minor* classic, as if its proper place were down in the foothills of the humour Everest). By holding Mr Pooter's immortal diary up to the distaff mirror, so to speak, I have attempted to show how that great wealth of absurd and touching minutiae may have looked from Mrs Pooter's point of view.

We know from the original source that Carrie is a woman of some independence of mind (MAY 30: 'Mrs James has more intellect in her little finger than both your friends have in their entire bodies'); that she possesses considerable spirit (MAY 9: 'Don't be theatrical, it has no effect on me. Reserve that tone for your new friend, *Mister* Farmerson, the ironmonger'); that her opinions of Charles Pooter and his doings stop far short of idolatry (APRIL 29: 'He tells me his stupid dreams every morning nearly'); but as often as not it is only Mr Pooter's evaluation of the day's events in the small world they share, with which we are favoured. What does Mrs Pooter make of it all? What does she really think of Charles Pooter's friends, his jokes, his job, his aspirations? What are *her* aspirations? How does Mrs Pooter spend her day while Mr Pooter is at the office? What is her real opinion of Holloway and 'The Laurels,' Brickfield Terrace? Such are the questions which I have diffidently – and affectionately – tried to answer.

A word to Pooter scholars about the Pooter calendar. In the original diary – possibly as a result of the confusion caused by the charwoman Mrs Birrell (sometimes spelled Mrs Birrel) having

11

torn out the entries between AUGUST 29 and OCTOBER 30 in which to wrap up kitchen scraps – NOVEMBER 5, which should be a Monday, is given as a Sunday. The diary remains a day out until mid-December, when – apart from one solitary lapse on JULY 3 – it reverts to the proper order. To avoid confusion among readers comparing day-by-day accounts of the same events in the two diaries, I have kept to the Pooter calendar in Mrs Pooter's diary.

I have the honour to be, Sir,

Yours & c & c

Keith Waterhouse

I have discovered (although he does not yet know that I know!) what it is that my husband does in the quarter-of-an-hour before retiring each night. If *he* may entertain hopes of publishing a diary, then so may *I* – after all, it is not as if my dear Charlie were a 'Somebody' whose thoughts and impressions are any more profound or worthwhile than the next person's. He is, alas, thanks to the good nature that holds him back, no more of a 'Somebody' than is –

MRS CHARLES POOTER

The Laurels,
   Brickfield Terrace,
      Holloway.

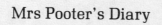

Mrs Pooter's Diary

Carrie

We move into our new home overlooking the railway, and I resolve to make the best of it. Mrs Borset leaves her card. I return her call and order some butter. The sash-cords go unattended to while Charles worries unduly about the scraper. We are snubbed by the Vicar.

'The Laurels'

1

My dear husband Charlie and I have just been a week in our new house, 'The Laurels,' Brickfield Terrace, Holloway.

I hate it. The back garden runs down to the railway, with the consequence that whenever a train passes by, the windows rattle (there is hardly a one that does not need new sash-cords) and smoke billows in through every crack, bringing with it an acrid stench which permeates my whole household. It is useless to scold Sarah (my maid) for cutting corners when, even after one of those rare mornings upon which she has set about her chores with a will, every stick of furniture is soon after coated in cinder-dust. As if that were not enough, there is evidence of rising damp in the scullery. All Charlie has to say on that score is that when we are settled in he may try his hand at growing mushrooms.

For a pound a year more we could have had a pretty little villa near our old home in Peckham, and with a bay window – but no, nothing would do but that my lord and master must be near to his precious City, at Mr Perkupp's beck and call. I wonder he does not take his bed down to the office and be done with it. It is not as if his loyalty and devotion to his duties ever met with appreciation – he lets himself be put upon and is too easy-going to push himself forward, that is Charlie's trouble, and that is why men with a tenth of his abilities have been promoted over his head.

When all's said and done, however, although he occasionally behaves oddly and says strange things, Charlie is in all other respects everything that a wife could wish for. He is a good husband to me and unlike other men does not pass the evening at his Club, but prefers to be at home with his pipe (ugh!), entertaining his friends (who call far too often for my liking) or doing jobs about the house. I must count my blessings. I know he will mend those sash-cords as soon as he has a mind to. I will say for the new house that it has a nice front breakfast-parlour where the trains could hardly be heard, if only they would not sound their whistles as they enter the Holloway tunnel. I shall continue to be a dutiful wife and make the best of things.

APRIL 3. I was writing my bi-weekly letter to our dear boy Willie, who is doing very well in the Bank at Oldham (he has all the 'drive' that his father lacks), when Sarah (my maid) brought in a card 'what a Lady 'ad left.' Our very first caller, and my domestic staff turn her away! Had the parlour bell not been broken, like much else in this house, I should have been aware that we had a visitor and given instructions that I was at home. I was chiding Sarah for her ignorance of 'the done thing' when she begged my pardon and explained that the front door was jammed, and that she had been in the act of stooping to address our caller through the letter box, asking her to be so good as to go round to the side door, when the card fluttered at her feet. It is one of our neighbours, a Mrs Borset, who so honours us. I shall return Mrs Borset's call at the earliest convenience.

APRIL 4. Consulted *Lady Cartmell's Vade Mecum For The Bijou Household*, which I am taking in as it appears in weekly parts, upon the etiquette of returning a call in a new locality. Unfortunately, since the last number brings the work only up to 'Ventilation, necessity of,' Lady Cartmell's observations on Visiting are yet to appear.

Trusting that I was not returning Mrs Borset's call too precipitously, I dressed suitably and sallied forth at what I judged to be the appropriate hour, to the address printed upon her card. This proved to be the Welsh Dairy on the corner, with, however, a residence above it. There being no private entrance that I could see, I was hesitating upon the pavement, wondering whether Lady Cartmell would advise in these circumstances entering the shop and instructing the butterman to inform his mistress that Mrs Pooter had called, when an upper window was thrown up and a lady wearing a mob-cap and night attire hailed me with the enquiry, Was I Mrs Pooter?

My hostess (as she announced herself to be) then apologised for not recognising me at once, saying that although I had been pointed out to her in the street (she did not volunteer by whom), I had not then been wearing what she was pleased to call 'all my finery'. Mrs Borset further apologised for being unable to receive me, as she was yet to complete her toilet, but if I would care to go into the shop, the assistant would be pleased to take my order, and I could rest assured that everything was fresh. I ordered some butter and eggs. So ended my first social engagement in Holloway.

APRIL 5. It is too bad of Charlie. Today, two shoulders of mutton arrived, he having arranged for another butcher without it ever entering his head that I might already have attended to this most elementary of household duties. Had my dear husband consulted me, or Part VI of *Lady Cartmell's Vade Mecum For The Bijou Household*, he would have learned that in the absence of a housekeeper, the ordering up of victuals (except table wines, porter and spirits) is the responsibility of the mistress. The piece ordered by me being the less fatty of the two, and not a few pence cheaper, his shall go back.

Altogether a vexing day. Following upon an uninvited, and to my mind premature visit, since we are not yet settled in, by Charlie's 'friend' Mr Cummings last even-

21

ing, his other 'friend' Mr Gowing called, equally uninvited, and for the second time this week. Mr Gowing made a song-and-dance about having tripped over our broken door-scraper – his own fault, for coming to the side-door (it may well be the case that the front door will not open, but he is not to know that). Charlie thereupon repeated an observation he had first made when Mr Cummings likewise fell over the scraper: that he must get it removed, or else he should get into a scrape. I expect he fears an action for damages could lie. I cannot understand why my husband fusses about the door-scraper, which to my mind is the landlord's responsibility, yet fails to concern himself with the faulty sash-cords, which render the necessary constant opening and closing of windows, to air the rooms as and when the trains go by, a danger to Sarah (my maid).

Mr Gowing

APRIL 6. Charlie in a filthy mood this morning. First, he took it into his head to declare his breakfast egg uneatable. I tasted it and could find nothing wrong with it. Nonetheless, I offered him mine – I had eaten but a spoonful – but no: he was adamant that Sarah (my maid) must return the eggs to Borset's, including, if you please, those already boiled and even our half-eaten ones! This is how he pays me back for ordering a shoulder of mutton over his head. It is very embarrassing for me, when Mrs Borset is so far my only social acquaintance in the district. (I am informed that our next-door neighbour is a Mrs Ledgard, and doubtless she is aware that I am Mrs Pooter, since our respective maids have 'exchanged credentials' over the back garden wall; but she has yet to call, although we have nodded to one another in the Terrace.)

Charlie then fell into a fury about his umbrella being missing (it was raining cats and dogs). Mr Gowing must have taken it by mistake, since according to Sarah he left his stick behind last evening. This pays my husband back on two accounts: for being so beastly at breakfast; and for allowing his friends to traipse in and out of the house as if it were a railway station – it may sound like one when the trains are passing, but I will not have it treated like one.

An uneventful day, most of the afternoon being taken up in unpacking my Gossware, a task I dare not entrust to Sarah, and arranging it on the parlour mantelpiece. Noted that although each piece was carefully wrapped in tissue-paper, a fine deposit of cinder-dust from the railway had insinuated itself into Aunt Rhoda's Great Yarmouth boot and the Blackpool perambulator presented to us by our thoughtful son Willie, while a small fragment of coal was lodged in my Broadstairs pie-funnel. This latter piece now furthermore sports a hair-crack extending half-way across the Broadstairs coat-of-arms, but the culprits in this case may be Messrs Carter Patterson's pantechnicon crew rather than the Directors of the Great Northern Railway.

23

Mr Cummings likewise fell over the scraper

This evening, hearing an altercation in the downstairs hall between Sarah and a tradesman, Charlie went out to investigate. He was gone some time, during which the commotion increased in volume. He came back looking very flushed but would say no more than that Mr Borset was to be given no further custom, nor were any of the blackguardly provision merchants in the Holloway Road with whom Mr Borset was in cahoots; but that in future I should give him my daily list of requirements in the way of dairy produce, and he would make himself responsible for purchasing eggs, butter and the remainder from Messrs Lipton's in the City Road, on his way home from the office. I held my peace.

APRIL 7. Being Saturday, I was suprised when Mrs Borset was announced by Sarah (my maid), for I have always understood that ladies do *not* pay calls at weekends. I had no sooner despatched Sarah across to Borset's (contrary to Charlie's instructions, this being the nearest shop) for a Madeira cake, than I learned that this was not, after all, a visit of a social nature. Mrs Borset had come round to prepare the ground for Mr Borset, who she said had 'had words' with my husband last evening in consequence of his having been out celebrating, and now wished to make amends with a pound of fresh butter and a sample packet of breakfast cocoa.

Sarah, who has yet to learn what the area steps are for, was just returning through the side door as I showed Mrs Borset out (the front door still refuses to open). Espying the Madeira cake in its paper bag stamped with an engraving of the Welsh Dairy, Mrs Borset exclaimed: 'O, I am glad you are still favouring us with your custom after all, Mrs Pooter. I should have fetched that over myself, had I known.'

This evening Mr Borset presented Charlie with the pound of butter but neglected to bring the sample packet of breakfast cocoa, about which omission I kept silent. Charlie was very pleased and announced that he had had second thoughts about making the detour to Lipton's two or three times a week, as it was not convenient for him. Good humour restored, he set to laying the old stair carpet we have fetched with us from Peckham. As I have been telling him all along, it is too narrow.

APRIL 8. To Church. Charlie full of himself because the Curate walked home with us and asked him to be a sidesman, which he takes as a great compliment. If it is so great a compliment, why does not the invitation extend from the Vicar – our intercourse with whom has so far been limited to the limpest of handshakes?

I engage extra staff. The hashed mutton comes to grief. My husband for once stands up for himself. The Misses Tipper inspect the house. Charlie instrumental in spoiling a batch of ladies' fingers, whose poor quality he then criticises. I worry about his drinking.

2

APRIL 9. Engaged a charwoman, a Mrs Birrell, on references supplied by Messrs Teale (late Moxon), painters' sundrymen, Sarah (my maid) claiming she is no longer able to manage the rough work. She managed it well enough in Peckham, although it has to be said that we were there blessed with an establishment well away from the railway-lines, where it was not a daily struggle to prevent the house from resembling a coal-siding.

Thus I have doubled my staff of domestics. I have arranged a system of bell-signals – one ring for Sarah, two for Mrs Birrell. That is, when the bells have been mended.

I fear Mrs Birrell's first impression of us will not have been a good one, for Charlie had to choose this morning to allow himself to be dragged into an absurd and unseemly slanging match with the butcher (his butcher, I should say), who came demanding to know why he has given back-word on the shoulder of mutton he ordered. Mrs Ledgard next door must have heard every word. Charlie tried to blame me for having put him in this position, but I would not have it. Furthermore, I warned him in no uncertain terms against entertaining hopes that his butcher is another Mr Borset, who will come running back cap in hand with a peace offering of brawn or suet.

APRIL 10. A disastrous day. Accompanying Sarah (my maid) into the kitchen, to taste the patent mushroom ketchup she wished to add to this evening's hashed mutton, I caught Cinders, the little cat which has adopted us, with her head in the stewpan. Sarah being a witness, who does not know when to hold her tongue, I had no alternative but to give our supper to Mrs Birrell. Anticipating the song-and-dance Charlie would make if denied his Tuesday hashed mutton, let alone how he would crow about the shoulder of mutton I had selected (in preference to his) being too small and fatty to meet our needs for the week, I sent Sarah out for a piece of best end of neck which I then made her turn into a hash. Charlie pronounced it the tastiest he has ever eaten, yet could not bring himself to admit that when it comes to buying mutton, the wiser head may be mine!

APRIL 11. The house reeks of paint, Charlie having elected to have the stairs entirely repainted, instead of merely that portion where the stair carpet does not meet the paintwork. He tells me that Mr Putley, the decorator he has engaged, 'has tramped all over North London trying to match the colour that is already down.' As it is dark chocolate, one of the commonest colours to be found, I beg leave to doubt this. I asked Charlie if Mr Putley has tried Messrs Teale (late Moxon), painters' sundrymen, who, by the look of their letterhead, seem reliable. He grew short-tempered and snapped that 'matching paint was men's business.'

APRIL 12. Saw Mrs Ledgard, our neighbour, in Balmforth's, the Chemists, where I was buying spermaceti and essential oil of almonds to make up into pomatum. Mrs Ledgard did not acknowledge my bow but it is probable that she did not see me, as she was preoccupied in inspecting camphor-balls.

Mr Gowing, who came round this evening to use my breakfast-parlour as his smoking-divan, had his 'come-uppance' from Charlie, I am pleased to say. Both he and Mr Cummings have been very tiresome about the smell of paint. On this occasion, as he began his usual sniffing, Charlie anticipated him by 'hoping he wasn't going to complain of the smell of paint again.' Upon Mr

Cummings saying: 'No, not this time; but I'll tell you what, I distinctly smell dry rot,' Charlie retorted, without pausing for an instant to compose his reply: 'You're talking a lot of *dry rot* yourself.' How we both roared at Mr Cummings' discomfiture. I was so proud of my dear Charlie: if only he would stand up for himself more often.

APRIL 13. The Misses Tipper, acquaintances from our Peckham days, came over to inspect the house. They contemplate moving to Holloway to be nearer their brother, who has a veterinary practice here. I put out the Madeira cake bought of Mrs Borset for her own consumption. How I now wish she had stayed to eat a crumb of it: for all that it has been kept in a tin with a tight lid, it was as dry as plaster of Paris.

The Misses Tipper were highly complimentary about 'The Laurels,' Miss Tipper Jnr being kind enough to say that 'I must have done wonders'. Miss Tipper Senr found Brickfield Terrace most agreeable but hoped that 'after all, Oswald [the brother] might be persuaded to transfer his veterinary practice to Peckham, sooner than put his sisters to the trouble of removing house'.

APRIL 14. My *Charlotte Russe* is a particular favourite with Charlie, as are the accompanying ladies' fingers which he will often take with his tea in preference to Marie Louise biscuits. He insists that my home-made ladies' fingers are superior to the bought-in variety; accordingly, although it is a fiddle-faddle for me, it was contentedly enough that I was applying myself to turning out a batch this afternoon, when I heard my husband calling urgently from the garden, where he was sowing half-hardy annuals. Thinking him to have had an accident – his 'green fingers' are all *thumbs*, I fear – I abandoned my whisking and stirring and hurried out.

All Charlie wanted of me was to listen to him say: 'I have just discovered we have got a lodging house. Look at the *boarders* (borders).' By the time I had given him a piece of my mind and returned to the kitchen, my ladies' fingers mixture was as stiff as custard. I should not have encouraged him by laughing at his joke about dry rot on Thursday: now he considers himself no end of a wit. In any case, my own play of words on green fingers and thumbs is as funny, if not funnier, but I should not be thanked for saying so.

Charlie drank a third of a bottle of whisky

APRIL 15. Charlie, having delivered himself of the opinion, after luncheon, that the *Charlotte Russe* was 'not up to scratch,' wisely took himself off for a long walk with his cronies. Spent a tranquil Sunday afternoon writing letters and perusing art silks in an old Liberty's catalogue. Listened to the hurdy-gurdy at the end of the street. Made a note to ask Sarah (my maid) to touch up the gilt on our pier-glasses with a bruised onion soaked in flour of sulphur. Did a little needle-work. Charlie did not return until well after tea-time – much to my disappointment, since he would have found a selection of stale Marie Louise biscuits most prettily arranged on a doily, as a change from his accustomed ladies' fingers.

APRIL 16. Reminded Charlie that although he has had a man in to repair his precious door-scraper, yet the sash-cords, bells and front door remain unattended to. He made a great show of examining the cords on the parlour windows, repeated 'Yes, I'm afraid they're frayed' several times with increasing emphasis, then took himself off into the garden, where I heard him laughing to himself.

I occasionally find myself wondering if the responsibilities and hardships of slaving under Mr Perkupp are turning my husband into a secret drinker. This morning I chanced to encounter Mrs Cummings outside the Fancy Bazaar, who confided that the reason our husbands and Mr Gowing and another drinking-companion were so late in returning from their walk yesterday, was that they had dallied at a public-house. Strange that Charlie, usually so meticulous in recounting every detail of his day, did not think to mention this!

APRIL 17. Went round myself to the ironmonger's and asked Mr Farmerson to attend to the sash-cords, the bells and the troublesome front door. He showed me where the jobs were down in his order-book, marked most urgent, 'as particularly requested by Mr Pooter,' and I was to take his word that they would have been executed at the same time as the other work, had it not been for the distraction of penetrating a gas-pipe when repairing the scraper. Upon hearing this explanation, I felt quite ashamed. I hope my impetuous visit to Farmerson's does not reach the ears of my husband.

APRIL 18. Announcing that he was in for a cold (I had not noticed it), Charlie drank a third of a bottle of whisky, aided and abetted by Mr Cummings. At least he is now doing his drinking in his own home, and does not make a secret of it.

My husband buys twelve bottles of whisky. Annie Fullers (now Mrs James, of Sutton) has melancholy news of the Bronchial Cigarillos failure. A successful dinner party, followed by a less than successful evening at the Tank Theatre. A tart exchange of letters with Mrs Ledgard. Charlie is aggravating with some paint.

3

APRIL 19. Mr Merton, a wine and spirits merchant, was introduced into the house by his friend Mr Cummings. After a few pleasantries of the most effusive 'buttering-up' variety, he proclaimed that Charlie too should be his friend, and that he would put him down for a dozen of his 'Lockanbar' whisky – 36s. and cheap at the price. Attempting a discreet intervention I said: 'Half a dozen would be even cheaper, and *to anyone seeing double* they would still look to be a dozen!' I hoped by my accompanying grimace to make it plain that this was no mere jest, but Mr Merton either did not comprehend or did not wish to, for he rejoined heartily: 'Ah, but Mr Pooter is like me – he does not go in for half-measures. When he puts his mind to a thing, he does so wholeheartedly!' Charlie simpered and nodded fit for his head to roll off. If he is about to make a habit of ordering whisky by the case, then we are done for. Meantime, there will be the worry of disposing of the empty bottles without Sarah (my maid) or Mrs Birrell apprehending what is going on.

APRIL 20. To tea with my old school friend Annie Fullers (now Mrs James, of Sutton), who is staying with her mother in Kennington while her husband attends to some business in Town. I am distressed to find Annie in straitened circumstances, being reduced to taking in sewing to make ends meet – 'obliging friends so as to keep my hands busy,' as she puts it. If I had known of her situation a week ago I could have asked her to make up my chair-covers, instead of getting a woman in. She keeps up a brave face, but reading between the lines, I gather that Mr James' venture into the field of Bronchial Cigarillos has not been attended with the success he had hoped for, and that he is now anxious to sell up and return to the coal business. It must be an anxious time for them: what a blessing that Annie is such a good needlewoman. I am quite shocked at Mr James' failure. How well I remember, upon Annie pointing out to me her husband's very first advertisement placard on the green 'Atlas' 'bus, my thrill of pride at having the right to count myself the oldest friend of the wife of – the Sole Proprietor of 'JAMES' CIGAR DE OZONE FOR THE RELIEF OF PHLEGM.' I shall say nothing of this to Charlie, since I have more than once held up Mr James as a model of enterprise and endeavour.

APRIL 21. A letter with an Oldham postmark, addressed to Mrs Ledgard, was mixed up in today's second post. I despatched Sarah (my maid) next door with it directly, with Mrs Pooter's compliments. I wonder what Mrs Ledgard's connexion is with Oldham; it is quite an amazing coincidence, our dear son Willie being in the Bank there. It will give our neighbour and myself a subject of conversation when we become acquainted.

Charlie's case of 'Lockanbar' delivered by handcart. I had half a mind to send it back, but he would only find some other means of obtaining what he must have. Upon returning from business he affected indifference towards the consignment's arrival, saying only: 'O, yes, I wondered when it would be despatched, as I already have Merton's invoice. By the by, he has sent us four seats for Monday's performance at the Tank Theatre, Islington.'

I should have put down in my diary that Charlie's new found friend having offered to let us have passes for any theatre in London, I had suggested to Charlie an evening at the play with Annie Fullers (now Mrs James, of Sutton) and Mr James while they are in Town. I was hoping for something nearer the Haymarket than Islington Green, but no matter, it will take Annie out of herself. Mr Merton has his uses for good, after all.

APRIL 22. At church, saw a lady who might have been a third Miss Tipper, but Charlie would not see the resemblance. Still no more than a handshake and a 'So pleased' from the Vicar.

Charlie took one glass of stout with luncheon, and nothing but water from the carafe with supper. Towards bedtime, however, he put aside the gardening manual he is forever conning these days, and said with studied offhandedness: 'I quite forgot to lay down Merton's whisky. I may as well do it now, before turning in.' With this, he took himself down to the cellar. I went up at five and twenty past ten. At eleven I was briefly aroused by the church clock, when I could hear him crashing about downstairs.

APRIL 23. As soon as Charlie set off for the City, I went down into the cellar. To my relief, the dozen of 'Lockanbar' lay undisturbed. Furthermore, what little quantity of whisky remained in the parlour decanter after Mr Merton's visit the other evening appeared untouched – I sniffed at it, and it did not have a diluted smell as if it had been watered. How I pray that I may have imagined a pernicious weakness where there was only a foolish one. Yet how must Charlie have been occupying himself until who knows what hour last night? Not in writing up his diary, to be sure – for I got it out of its hiding-place and *yesterday is blank*!

My mind set comparatively at rest, I was then able to direct my attention to the arrangements for Dinner, to which Annie Fullers (now Mrs James, of Sutton) and Mr James are invited, before the theatre this evening. It will be our first dinner party in our new home, thus I am anxious that everything must be just so. After consulting with *Lady Cartmell's Vade Mecum For The Bijou Household*, I have arranged a menu as follows:

39

First course
Gravy soup
Entrée
Croquettes of mutton

Second course
Cold broiled beef
with
oyster sauce
Mashed potatoes   Bottled beetroot
Boiled onions

Third course
Compôte of rhubarb
Ladies' fingers
Dessert
Café

Spent the entire day preparing the meal with the assistance of Sarah (my maid), Mrs Birrell, and Mrs Birrell's daughter Evangeline, whom she is keeping away from the ragged school with anaemia. Was too exhausted to dare rest before changing, for I should have nodded off, and so wrote up this my diary.

Later: The dinner party was a great success, spoiled only by Charlie's murmured congratulations upon 'an excellent meat tea'. I wish I could say as much for the theatrical portion of the evening. Having reached the Tank Theatre, Islington – a low place, so I feared Annie and Mr James would regard it, little better than a music-hall – there was a mix-up over the tickets, Mr Merton's pass having been issued by a previous management. While Charlie was arguing fruitlessly with the gentleman who barred our way, Mr James slipped away and returned with a ticket for Box H, which he had calmly bought and paid for himself. This with all the calls upon his purse due to the failure of his Bronchial Cigarillos manufactory! And after he had already paid our fares on two 'buses, insisting that it was enough that Charlie had bought the theatre tickets! I was never so humiliated, and could not look Annie in the face.

Worse was to come. Reaching the box, we found that Mr James had purchased two silk programmes, which were laid out for us where we were to sit. I tried to signal Charlie with my eyes to offer at least to pay for these, but he was too occupied in fiddling with the ridiculous patent bow tie he had on (and which later fell into the pit). In the Ladies' withdrawing-room during the first interval, Annie was near to tears. 'Next, he will want to stand everyone water-ices, and this is how he carries on!' she almost sobbed. 'He will have us bankrupt before he is done! Were it not for my needle we should not have

Fiddling with the ridiculous patent bow-tie he had on

a roof over our heads!' I had no money with me, and so could not offer to pay our share of the evening's expenses myself. I pressed poor Annie's hand, and promised to visit her very soon, in Sutton, fetching with me seven yards of cretonne to be made up into curtains for our dear son Willie's room (in the home he is yet to see!).

APRIL 24. Returning to 'The Laurels' from a short afternoon walk to try out my new glaze button boots (they will have to be stretched), whom should I encounter passing our gate but Mrs Ledgard. In view of having done her a small service, by sending her mis-directed letter across on Saturday, I felt emboldened to speak. I said: 'Good morning,' (recollecting later that it was not morning) 'I trust you received your letter from Oldham, which was wrongly delivered to "The Laurels"?' Mrs Ledgard said, 'Yes, thank you – *eventually*,' and walked on without bowing.

APRIL 25. Sarah (my maid) having stayed over at her married sister's in The Borough on her afternoon off yesterday, it was not until today that I could enquire what light she might be able to throw upon Mrs Ledgard's strange remark. Sarah was most positive that she had hurried next door with the letter 'the minute you put it in me 'and, mum'; Mrs Ledgard's maid had thanked her, and promised to take it in to her mistress at once, as it would be from her cousin, from whom she was expecting news of her niece's success or otherwise in the ladies' violin competition at the Oldham Musical Festival. It is a puzzle. Accordingly, I sat down and penned the following, and sent Sarah across with it: 'Mrs Charles Pooter presents her compliments, and should Mrs Ledgard be under the misapprehension that her letter was in any way delayed, would respectfully draw attention to the fact that it was postmarked "Oldham, 7.30pm, Apl 20" and was sent across to Mrs Ledgard most promptly, after arriving by the second post on Apl 21.' I added what, in a less formal note, would have been

42

a PS.: 'By a strange coincidence, Mrs Pooter's son is at Oldham, where he has a place in Throstle & Epps' Linen Bank.'

Beside myself with rage this evening. His Lordship came home bearing two tins of Pinkford's red enamel paint, as advertised. Asked where he had bought them, he replied: 'O, I was recommended, *I forget by whom*, to look in Teale's (late Moxon), painters' sundrymen. They have a very good range, and it is too bad that Putley didn't look there when trying to match our paint, before putting me to the expense of redecorating.' I could barely speak. Later he called me out to the garden to admire some flower-pots he had painted, quite unnecessarily. I said ironically: 'If there was one job about the house I wanted you to do above all others, it was to paint the flower-pots.' As usual, he took my sarcasm for praise, and looked so pleased with himself that my heart melted, and I said with a shake of my head: 'You've always got some new-fangled craze,' then returned indoors, leaving him painting a brick. Later Sarah (my maid) complained that he had gone into her room without her leave and painted her washstand, towel-horse and chest-of-drawers. If Sarah gives notice I shall paint his head.

APRIL 26. An extraordinary missive from Mrs Ledgard, pushed through the letterbox. It reads: 'Dear Madam, as you appear to be in the habit of reading *other people's postmarks*, you are very well placed to know that my letter from Oldham was posted in ample time to be wrongly delivered to you *by the first post* the following morning. Had it been redirected straight away, and not after the *second post* had been and gone, I should have been spared much anxiety. Yours &c Ruby Ledgard.' It is easy to see that her niece in Oldham was not successful in the violin competition, and so she is venting her disappointment upon me. I shall not reply.

43

APRIL 27. Sharp words with Charlie, who has now painted the bath red without consulting me. I have never heard of such a thing as a vermillion bath. However, it is quite obvious to me, as it would be to him if he would only read the instructions on the tin before painting everything in sight, that Pinkford's being so emphatic that their enamel paint must be applied to a cold surface and is not recommended for stoves or grates, it must either flake or dissolve when brought into contact with scalding water. The bath will then look such a sight that Charlie will have to ask Farmerson's to come in and paint it white – exactly as he should have done in the first place. Accordingly, beyond remarking that having tardily discovered the merits of Messrs Teale (late Moxon), it was a pity he could not obtain some Flack's Leather Reviver (available of all painters' sundrymen) and restore my worn writing-case and blotter, I was content to let the matter drop.

If any rancour remained, it evaporated completely when I heard Charlie's droll obversation to Mr Gowing and Mr Cummings, apropos their constant traipsing in and out of my parlour as if it were their own: 'Doesn't it seem odd that Gowing's always *coming* and Cummings always *going*?' They were *not* amused. I fancy we shall enjoy less of their company in future.

As for my new glaze button boots, they are much more comfortable.

A proud day in our lives. Mrs Shrike, of Bow, calls unexpectedly, owing to sudden faintness resulting from weak blood. Failure of usual remedies to remove a port stain. I am forced to deceive my husband. A dress fitting in Sutton. The Ball at the Mansion House.

4

APRIL 30. The proudest day of my life. An invitation has arrived from the Lord and Lady Mayoress of London, bidding us to a Reception at the Mansion House, on Monday, May 7. I could scarcely take it in, and had to read the inscription several times before it would stop dancing before my eyes.

The card is addressed, as is only right and proper, to 'Mr and Mrs Charles Pooter,' but it is to my dear Charlie alone that the City extends this signal honour. Here is proof, if proof were needed, that however humiliatingly he may be trampled upon in Mr Perkupp's office, by men not fit to clean his boots, my husband's excellence of character, his steadfastness of purpose, his application and industry, his reputation for honest dealing, in short, his sovereign worth, do not go unnoticed by our men of affairs in their clubs and chop-houses.

Ever modest – if only he were less so! – Charlie would not indulge himself in a moment's self-congratulation upon the esteem in which he is held. Rather was *his* pride in *me*, as he anticipated his presenting 'My dear, pretty wife' (his very words) to the Lord and Lady Mayoress at the Mansion House. We said such tender things to one another then, that my eyes filled with tears. We have not spoken so since we were on our honeymoon at Deal.

I shall want a new silk dress, court gloves, fan, Dolly Varden dress shoes, stockings, evening bag, jet combs, and the Madeira lace shawl I have seen in Shoolbred's, but otherwise, I will make do with what I have got.

Mrs Shrike, of Bow

MAY 1. A Mrs Shrike called. Thinking her to be one of our neighbours, I spoke generally of Brickfield Terrace, and then asked politely whether she lived on our side of the street that backs onto the railway, or no. To this, Mrs Shrike replied: 'O, there is no railway near where I live, that I know of.' It then came out that Mrs Shrike is from Bow, but has a brother in Coppernail Terrace (the next street but four), whom she was on her way to visit when she felt suddenly faint, and so thought to ring our doorbell. Mrs Shrike has weak blood, which precipitates these attacks from time to time, when she must sit down.

Knowing that the doctor prescribes port wine for Evangeline Birrell, my charwoman's daughter, who suffers from anaemia, I invited Mrs Shrike to take a glass with her tea and ladies' fingers, which she gratefully accepted. By way of a conversation piece, I showed her our invitation to the Lord and Lady Mayoress's reception; it greatly impressed her and I believe helped her to feel better, for soon she declared herself much recovered and was on her way.

As Sarah (my maid) was clearing away the tea things, I noticed that Mrs Shrike had carelessly put down her empty port glass on top of the invitation card, which, instead of returning to the mantelpiece, I had foolishly left on the lacquer and mother-of-pearl side table. Sarah picking up the glass, the invitation card adhered to its base; whereat, as I reached out to retrieve the precious and – as I thought – pristine pasteboard rectangle, I saw, to my horror, a sticky, dark red ring where the port glass had rested.

Cold water applied with a handkerchief would not remove the blemish; nor hot water applied with butter muslin; nor chloride of soda; nor common soap; nor Neave's Varnish Stain Remover; nor purified bullock's blood; nor essence of lemon. Rectified spirits of wine only made the wine stain worse. I bundled Sarah off to Balmforth's, the Chemist's, for fuller's earth, a small bottle of sulphuric ether and anything else they might recommend; but before she had time to get back, I heard Charlie's key in the latch. With an inspiration born from terror I swept the mutilated invitation into an envelope from my writing case, together with a letter I had already written to Mother, giving her our important news; I sealed it hurriedly, and was addressing it with trembling hand as Charlie came into the parlour. In as bright a voice as I could muster, I asked his leave to send the invitation to Mother to look at. Charlie put his arm around my quaking shoulders and said: 'Of course you may! I want all the world to know that my little wife is invited to the Mansion House. . . Why, Carrie, my love, you're crying!'

MAY 2. Devoted much of the day to reading up my back numbers of *Lady Cartmell's Vade Mecum For The Bijou Household* on matters of dress, etiquette, forms of address and the remainder. Lady Cartmell is silent on

49

the subject of removing port stains from pasteboard, but I did turn up a recipe for Indian Trifle I had overlooked, and copied it out onto a half-sheet of notepaper which I put behind the clock. Also copied out the mode of replying to an invitation from a baronet (as the Lord Mayor is), which does *not* accord with the 'penny plain' style of reply drafted, at Charlie's solicitation, by Mr Perkupp. My thanks for this service was a curt: 'I'm sure Mr Perkupp knows best, Carrie, and anyway it is too late now.' So the paragon Mr Perkupp now knows better than Lady Cartmell how to address a baronet!

MAY 3. By train to Sutton, to consult with Annie Fullers (now Mrs James) about my dress for next Monday. Annie was insistent that she would be most offended if I did not allow her to make the dress herself, even though it will mean engaging a seamstress and working night and day. She showed me some plates from recent numbers of *The Queen* and *Daintrey's Illustrated Boudoir*, and we agreed upon the one Annie likes best, the 'Duchess of Albany' ball-gown, which she assures me is not too décolleté for the season. The price Annie quoted was a little higher than I had meant to pay, but it is a pleasure to be able to help my old school friend in her hour of need. Charlie must not know of our arrangement.

I found Annie much more composed. Seemingly Mr James is still hard-pressed, but he lives in hopes that the manufacturers of 'Fancy Joys' aromatic cigarettes will buy him out, although at a considerable loss to himself. I was allowed a peep into the nursery, where in view of Mr James' business anxieties, let alone considerations of dietary and digestion, I was surprised to behold little Percy (their only child) helping himself from a drum of 'Nonfinah' sugar damsons – just about the most expensive confectionary there is. It was not for me to remark on what I took to be yet another example of Mr James' profligacy; but Annie must have read the look on my face, for she laughed and said: 'O, he is only being allowed to finish what is left in the box! And you needn't be alarmed on my account, Carrie – I bought those myself, out of the deposit on five sailor dresses I am making for the Upcott girls at the Rectory.'

MAY 4. Mother, in returning the Lord Mayor's invitation, wrote that 'it was a pity about the smudge, and was this a sample of Charles' famous red enamel paint?' I burned her letter, and propped the disfigured card back on the parlour mantelpiece. Charlie, coming down to breakfast, espied it at once and, naturally, demanded an explanation. My invented apologies from Mother, for returning the card in such a state, so angered him that he left the house with scarcely another word. I was relieved at not having to elaborate my fabrications further, for I find it hateful to deceive my husband. Bad enough already, that the dress which Annie Fullers (now Mrs James, of Sutton) is making for me, I shall have to pretend is bought of W. P. & J. Hulkingson's Successors, of 9, 11 and 13 Milk Street, E.C.

MAY 5. Back to Sutton for a fitting, thence to Swan and Edgar's, Basnett et Cie, Shoolbred's, the Fancy Bazaar, and Jay's Mourning House (for the jet combs). After asking me in a tired voice whether I needs must have *everything* new for the only visit I am ever likely to make to the Mansion House in my life, my generous and unselfish husband produced from paper bags a new pair of lavender kid-gloves for himself, and *two* white ties. Does he intend to wear one about each ear?

MAY 6. Sunday. Usual dull sermon, followed by usual limp handshake. I asked the Vicar: 'Shall we be seeing you at the Mansion House reception tomorrow, Vicar?' He looked startled, and could only stammer: 'Alas, no, dear lady, I have other engagements.' Charlie confessed afterwards that he was hard put to keep a straight face.

MAY 7. *Engagements for this evening*: 10 o'c, Reception by the Worshipful the Lord and Lady Mayoress of

51

London, at the Mansion House, to meet the Representatives of Trades and Commerce.

How am I to squeeze such a red-letter day into one page of my scribbling diary? I must crab my hand, and be as concise as I may.

A.F. (now Mrs J.) came up early from Sutton & stitched all day with help of S. (my maid), while I returned to Basnett & Cie to exchange shoes, Swan & Edgar's to exchange gloves, &c &c. Gown more décolleté than I recall from fashion plate, but against this am able to remind C. that I have selected his favourite colour, sky-blue (A.F.'s original choice of salmon-pink being unobtainable in silk). Headache after luncheon, so lay on bed for a while with cold compress, made up of cucumber juice, to aid complexion whilst relieving pain.

4 o'c: Bath. 4.30 o'c: Tea off tray. Cucumber sandwiches dry, thanks to extraction of juice. 5 o'c: Tried pot of complexion improver & Crayon Rubens eyebrow pencil belonging to A.F. Scrubbed face & fell back upon my tried & trusted 'Poudre d'Amour' toilet powder. Words with A.F. for calling me 'a stick-in-the-mud'.

5.30 o'c: S. put up my hair. 6.0 o'c: A.F. re-arranged my hair. Words with S. for banging down water jug & slamming door. 6.30 o'c: vacated bedroom so that C. could get dressed, & spent ½ hr with jewellery case in parlour, arguing with A.F. as to what I should wear. Finally borrowed her drop ear-rings & seed-pearl choker. Also rehearsed reception by Lord & Lady Mayoress: felt silly curtseying to A.F. in undergarments.

7 o'c: Commenced to dress, while C. made nuisance of himself falling over, bleeding, getting coal-black dust on dress shirt &c &c. A.F. disapproved of little white fan, so produced from portmanteau her own priceless fan of Kachu eagle feathers. A.F. so v. kind to her friend. Begged her to let C. think she has also lent my Madeira lace shawl, in case he has seen its twin in Shoolbred's window & knows it cost 1 gn. 9 o'c: Descended to drawing room, where C. most lavish in his compliments,

*Bewigged footman looked sneeringly
at the port-stained invitation*

except on subject of fan, voicing preference for the one I showed him from Shoolbred's costing 7/6 (told him 3/6). Both A.F. and I sharp with him.

Cab to Mansion House. Bewigged footman looked sneeringly at port-stain on invitation. Forgot to curtsey to Lord Mayor, in agitation at wondering if he remembered C. as person who sent incorrect acceptance of same, acting upon faulty guidance of Mr Perkupp. Few other guests being yet present, had opportunity for conversation with Lady Mayoress, whilst C., perfectly at his ease, talked with Lord Mayor. Lady Mayoress kindly enquired as to whether we had come far, & upon being told Holloway, asked if we knew Dr & Mrs Ijow. Avowed we did, as can at least claim to have seen Dr Ijow's nameplate.

As crowds began to arrive, compared appearances & concluded that my dress held its own against all but the grandest, & was *not* too low-cut, despite what C. may think. Considered it a pity we didn't know anybody, & repeated this thought to C., until he replied: 'I wish you would stop saying that, Caroline. In any case, isn't that Mr Franching, from Peckham?' I never met a Mr Franching when we lived in Peckham, & had to seize C. by the coat-tails to prevent him going up to him & leaving me.

Spent as much time as was able dallying in supper room, noting that C. was drinking one glass of champagne after another. This on top of what he must have had at home, to make him fall over & tear leg of his dress trousers. Should have had all this out with him when he bought that case of 'Lockanbar' whisky. Not surprisingly, evening now began to deteriorate. Averting my eyes for only a moment in order to deal with a boiled custard, I addressed word to C. only to discover that he had deserted me & was chinking glasses across room with Mr Farmerson, our ironmonger, & a gentleman in Court uniform. Stared at him until he had the grace to return to my side, when, after swilling more champagne, he tried to make it up to me by asking me in most unctuous terms to dance. He could hardly see, let alone dance, & in no time at all he had me over, grazing my elbow & breaking one of my jet combs, new from Jay's Mourning Warehouse. There was a roar of laughter & I wished floor would swallow me up. A gentleman named Mr Darwitts helped me up & escorted me for a restoring sip of wine, while C. was brought back to his senses by his fine friends. Mr Darwitts most polite & considerate, & talked easily of this & that as if incident had never happened. He used to own a bookbindery in Cornhill, in partnership with his brother, but has relinquished his share of business & is now in wholesale stationery line.

Far from having learned his lesson, found C. still imbibing coarsely with Mr Farmerson, & it took a tap on his shoulder with A.F.'s Kachu eagle-feather fan to remind him that his wife was present, & that it was time to take our leave. Mr Farmerson insisted on sharing our cab. Of journey home, what with stench of tobacco smoke & Mr Farmerson knocking A.F.'s fan out of my hand as I tried to waft away fumes, & Charlie badgering him to come in for a nightcap of 'Lockanbar' whisky, despite my steely reminder that the hour was late, & Mr Farmerson not offering a farthing towards his share of cab, I shall say nothing.

After the Mansion House Ball. A chance meeting with Mr Darwitts. I take refuge at Sutton. A formal visit from Mrs Ledgard. I put my foot down over Belgian hare rabbits.

5

MAY 8. Settled up with Annie Fullers (now Mrs James) before her return to Sutton. Had meant to make up the discrepancy between the cost of my dress and what my husband believes it to have cost, from my pin money and the coal money in equal proportions; but after his behaviour last night I simply marched up and thrust a good half of the household bills at him, uttering boldly: 'I am badly out of pocket over *my* expenses for *your* entertaining evening at the Mansion House, and so you may settle these.' The poor man, who was looking very white this morning, took them like a lamb. If he thought, however, that I had done with him, that was his mistake! This evening, unable to eat the supper prepared for him (cold veal rolls with fat bacon and forcemeat; brown gravy) he came out with some cock-and-bull tale about 'being poisoned by the lobster mayonnaise last night.' I retorted: 'Champagne never did agree with you!' and thereupon put away my sewing and went to bed, leaving him spluttering his excuses to himself.

MAY 9. Had it out with Charles. I would have preferred to have let the subject of the Mansion House Ball drop, since no good ever came of protracted recriminations; but he was the one who had to bring it up, by demanding 'an explanation', if I pleased, of 'my conduct last night.' *My* conduct! I left him in no doubt as to what I thought of *his* conduct of the night before – his tippling, his reeking tobacco, his ill-judged choice of friends – and the way he allows them to use him as a doormat, in my presence

59

– his deficiencies as a husband and as a gentleman – with particular reference to his leaving it to Mr Darwitts to assume responsibility for me in my distress – and his behaviour generally. He fell into a sulk and would not answer.

MAY 10. Charlie still sulking. He can be like a child sometimes, and I told him as much.

MAY 11. To the Fancy Bazaar, to look at the new umbrella covers, whereby one's umbrella may be converted into a sunshade in an instant. A tall, very straight-backed gentleman, standing by the stationery counter, raised his hat and hoped 'I was quite recovered.' It was none other than Mr Darwitts. We shook hands and talked for a moment, but then Mr Darwitts had to attend to his business. He was hoping to interest the Fancy Bazaar in a line of correspondence

Mr Darwitts

cards in delicate colours, with rounded edges − a cut above the common-or-garden postcard, as he said.

Over supper I told Charles of my encounter with Mr Darwitts, adding: 'I had not realised he was so tall. He has the bearing of a cavalry officer.'

Charles said: 'A colour-sergeant would be nearer the mark, from what I recall.'

I said: 'Which can be precious little, after what you had to drink that night.'

Charles said: 'I would rather not go into that again, *if* it's all the same to you, Caroline,' and attended to his mutton pie. I thought of more cutting remarks, but kept them to myself.

MAY 12. My husband now in a pet because the *Blackfriars Bi-weekly News*, having in the first place omitted our names from the list of guests at the Mansion House Ball, now has us down in its *addendum* as 'Mr and Mrs C. Porter'. I blame Charlie's illegible signature, when he wrote drawing the Editor's attention to the oversight. Mrs Birrell has a better hand, as I told him. This led to a further outburst. He said: 'I will have you know, Caroline, that Mr Perkupp considers my copperplate the best in the office.' I said: 'We are not discussing your precious Mr Perkupp, or your precious copperplate, but your absurd signature.'

Ever since reading in *The Strand* that 'a man's signature is a calligraphical portrait of his character,' he has been forever scribbling his name on scraps of paper − I find them crumpled up in the coal-scuttle − adding here a flourish, and there a curlicew, until his signature now resembles that of Charles Dickens in our 'Autograph' edition of the *Complete Works*.

Charles said: 'Whatever the subject, the discussion is at an end,' and left the room. He is very proud of that signature.

We cannot go on like this. It will be better for both of us that I should go and stay in Sutton with Annie Fullers (now Mrs James) for a spell, as she is always pressing me

. . . and thus we have been occupied night and day
(not excluding Sunday)

to do, until the storm-clouds have blown over. I sent off a telegram and packed. Overhearing me, as I instructed Sarah (my maid) on what to look for in a knuckle of veal, Charlie said: 'Don't worry about me – I can always dine at the Club.' He will have to join one first.

MAY 18. In the week of my stay with Annie Fullers (now Mrs James) at Sutton, I have had scarcely a moment to call my own, let alone in which to keep up this diary. A scrawled postcard to Charlie, reminding him that most of his collars are with the laundress, has been the extent of my literary effusions.

Arriving on the afternoon of last Saturday, I commenced, whilst Annie helped me to unpack, an account of the difficult patch I am going through with Charlie. To my dismay, my dear friend began to weep copiously. I said: 'There, Annie, it's not as bad as that! He will come round as he always does, and everything will be as right as rain!' Annie wailed: 'O, Carrie — it's not that — I don't know what to do! I know you have your troubles but mine are worse!' Through her sobs, she then unburdened herself. Having taken money from the Rector to make five sailor dresses for his daughters, she had fallen behind with the work, consequent upon her putting everything aside to make my 'Duchess of Albany' ball-gown, as a favour to me. A Mrs Dalfbrace had sent round a note this morning (Annie showed me a tear-stained rag of paper), to say that 'if Mrs James was unable to effect the alterations to her shot silk and velvet costume, and re-trim her black silk dolman, by mid-week, as faithfully promised, then Mrs Dalfbrace regretted she would have to make other arrangements.' Annie must either return the Rector's money for the five sailor dresses, which she had already spent, or give Mrs Dalfbrace backword, thereby losing her goodwill and that of her friends. There were bills to be paid. She could not turn to Mr James, whose dwindling capital was tied up in his Bronchial Cigarillos. They would be ruined.

I put my arm around Annie's shoulders and comforted her, reminding her that a trouble shared was a trouble halved. Soon, Annie and I were working tranquilly side by side, I taking up the hem and sleeves of Mrs Dalfbrace's costume, Annie cutting out sailor dresses from a bolt of linen. And thus we have been occupied, night and day (not excluding Sunday!).

MAY 21. Whilst attempting to snatch a few minutes' respite in another exhausting day, I was put to the embarrassment of being witness to a domestic fracas at Annie's tea-table.

Mr James, although still hardly knowing where his

63

next penny is coming from (the 'Fancy Joys' aromatic cigarette company is driving a hard bargain, I am given to understand), arrived back from business with an electro-plated self-pouring teapot that had caught his eye in a shop window. If he thought Annie would be pleased, he was mistaken. Refusing even to allow him to demonstrate the machine, and at least determine whether it was value for money or no (he said six shillings, but we have all played that trick), his little wife launched, in front of me, upon a tirade about his spending what they hadn't got, how they would end their days in the poor house, and such and so on. Annie's parting shot, as she swept out of the drawing room, was: 'Well, sir, two can play at that game!'

I hardly knew where to look. Mr James, perhaps to alleviate my confusion, made himself very busy in pouring the contents of teapot, kettle and slop-basin into the self-pouring device he had brought in, but failed to elicit any return of the liquid upon turning the tap. Through the window, I saw Annie storming down the path with her hat at a rakish angle, waving her parasol at a passing hansom cab. Necessity for some strained intercourse with Mr James was obviated, to my relief, by the fetching in of Master Percy, who was dandled upon his father's knee and given fruit-cake, whilst I attended to some sewing from Annie's work box. Presently, Annie came back into the room as abruptly as she had left it, with the announcement: 'You may pay off my cab, then carry the sewing machine up to my room.'

Mr James seemed dazed. 'Sewing machine, old girl? What sewing machine?'

'The sewing machine I have just bought on our account at Medlicott's, John – yes, the same place where you got your *seven-and-sixpenny* self-pouring teapot!'

MAY 22. Annie is as remarkable a woman as she was a schoolgirl. Within an hour, this morning, she had mastered the new machine. Within two, she had taught me how to use it. It is the 'Magician' model, which makes 1,000 stitches a minute. I began to make short work of the last of the sailor dresses for the Rector's daughters, whilst Annie sat down and wrote letters to all her friends, to acquaint them with her new toy. 'Mark my words, Carrie,' said Annie, pausing for a moment from her labours. 'Six months from now I shall have three of these machines, with women to work them!' I don't doubt that she will. For my own part, I look forward no farther than two days from now, when I shall have finished the curtains we are making for I know not whom, and I can get back to my little house in Brickfield Terrace.

MAY 24. Home sweet home again! How small 'The Laurels' seems by the side of the James' villa in Sutton; but I would not change my dear little home for the world (unless Charlie would agree to return to Peckham). The house looks not much the worse for my absence, and Charlie has at last had our Views of the Pyramids framed and hung them along the first landing, where they look very pretty. He says I have 'caught the sun.' I should like to know where I have caught it, not having set foot out of doors in a fortnight!

Threw out all the dead flowers, and had to cut fresh ones for myself, since no-one else has done it.

MAY 25. Mrs Ledgard, our neighbour, paid a call at last, but would not sit down, as 'what she had to say could be better said from the upright position, thank you.'

Mrs Ledgard said: 'I believe in live and let live, Mrs Pooter, and I consider myself to have been most tolerant whilst you were settling into your new home, when a certain amount of hammering and shifting of heavy objects is only to be expected. However, you will forgive me for saying that it has gone on beyond the bounds of reason – most certainly so when I have to put up with bangings and thuddings well after midnight. I am a widow, Mrs Pooter, and I must have my sleep.'

65

Although failing to understand the connexion between Mrs Ledgard's unfortunate widowhood and her needs for the arms of Morpheus, I was forced to the realisation that a good deal of noise *has* been made whilst we have been getting ship-shape, the more so since Charlie is never happier than when tapping at tin-tacks with his hammer. I apologised, and assured our neighbour that having got the last of our pictures hung, that should be the end of the nocturnal bangings. Mrs Ledgard replied that she hoped so, declining, however, my invitation to the first landing to inspect the Views of the Pyramids which are the gravamen of her complaint. This was perhaps fortunate, for now that I examine them more closely, I perceive that they are hung askew, with nail-holes in the wallpaper marking unsuccessful efforts to get them in true with one another.

MAY 26. Yesterday Charlie repeated his strange remark of some weeks ago, 'I'm afraid they're frayed' – this time in connexion with shirt-cuffs rather than the sash-cords (which are now as satisfactory as they will ever be, with our ill-fitting windows). He then laughed maniacally. I, at his urging, dutifully joined in his mirth.

This peculiar behaviour, combined with my suspicions that my husband must have hung our Views of the Pyramids when in drink, led me to his stock of 'Lockan-bar' as soon as he had gone out. The dozen bottles remain untouched and gathering dust. I cannot imagine what induced him to buy them.

JUNE 7. Too occupied and run off my feet to keep up with my diary, as Sarah (my maid) is taking her annual holiday. Seemingly oblivious of this fact, His Lordship chose to roll home in a hansom cab, with his friend Mr Franching, to take 'pot-luck.' I was very cool, and should have remained so, but for the circumstance that Mr Franching hails from Peckham. He knows the Misses Tipper by sight, and is acquainted with Mr Sumpter, of the Peckham Harriers, whom *we* know by sight, and so, with our having so much in common, a pleasant evening was passed after all.

JULY 7. If *my trusting husband* is given to secretly reading my diary, as I sometimes suspect, then he will have had a dull month of it. There has been no entry in his own diary for these past four weeks, therefore there is none in mine, either. If he is growing weary of recording his daily doings, then why should I persevere in recording mine – the more particularly since I have had nothing to set down beyond the daily arrival and departure times of Mr Cummings and Mr Gowing, who use this house as their Club? In future, I shall record only events of extraordinary interest.

JULY 8. Bought some of the new fashionable correspondence cards, in salmon pink and lemon, at the Fancy Bazaar. Informed by the assistant that they are 'all the go.' Mr Darwitts must be well satisfied.

JULY 19. After an unusual silence, Charlie said: 'I have half a mind to keep Belgian hare rabbits.'
  I said: 'Only a man with half a mind would think of such a stupid idea.' He buried himself in his *Exchange and Mart*, and did not utter another word the whole evening.

JULY 20. His diary continues to be a succession of blank pages. If, in the half hour or so when he pretends to be secretly writing up his diary, he is not secretly drinking, and he is not secretly reading *my* diary (I have stuck a few pages lightly together with a touch of Prout's Elastic Glue, and they remain undisturbed), then what is he about? I should dearly like to know.

JULY 27. Have spent half the week hunting high and low for a copy of *On The Stage And Off*, by Jerome K Jerome, which our dear son Willie has most particularly requested for his birthday; but it cannot be found for

67

We continued thus . . . until very late

love nor money. The volume cannot be ordered, as it is
out of print. I wonder if an ivory-handled razor would do
as well? I have seen a very nice one in Balmforth's, the
Chemist's, in its own case. Throsbourne & Argyll have
The Diary of A Pilgrimage, by the same author, which
they most warmly recommend, but I do not think it will
suit. It looks as if I shall have to make the journey to
Mudie's.

JULY 29. Have found out what he is up to. Last night I
came downstairs for a glass of water, the bedside bottle
being empty (*mem:* speak to Sarah (my maid)). I discovered him sitting at the dining table in his shirt
sleeves, with a large sheet of graph paper in front of him,
on which he was drawing with the aid of a ruler. It was
fruitless for him to try and hide his handiwork, and I had
no difficulty in reading the lettering he had inked in
along the top of the sheet: 'Elevation & Plan for a Hutch
to House 12 Belgian Hare Rabbits. Scale: ¼in = 1ft.'

I said: 'On the day twelve rabbits enter this house,
Charles, I shall leave it.'

He said: 'They will not be in the house, they will be in
the garden.'

I said: 'Are you insane? What do you suppose Mrs Ledgard will have to say when she sees that her neighbours have turned their back garden into a poultry yard?'

He said: 'Rabbits are not poultry. If only you would read the *Exchange and Mart*, Carrie, and see what Belgian hare rabbits are fetching these days! Quite apart from the money, and the little luxuries it would buy, every man should have his hobby.'

I said: 'Yes, and yours is hammering nails at all hours! Passers-by must think this is a cobbler's shop!' We continued thus, until very late, when there was a banging on the party wall, presumably with Mrs Ledgard's poker.

JULY 31. Evidently feeling contrite at the succession of quarrels and arguments we have been having lately, Charlie bought me a pretty silver bangle, and left it on my dressing table with an affectionate little note. He is a dear old thing at heart, and I shall make an effort to be nicer to him. Secured a copy of *On The Stage And Off*, and posted it to Oldham, marked 'Not to be opened until Thursday.' The only stiff wrapping paper I could find was the 'Elevation & Plan for a Hutch to House 12 Belgian Hare Rabbits.'

The return of our dear son, Willie Lupin Pooter, to the bosom of his family. A proud day for his mother. Our annual holiday, and my thoughts on 'good old' Broadstairs. A reunion with our long-lost (!) friends, Mr Cummings and Mr Gowing.

6

AUGUST 4. A red-letter day. No sooner had I read our dear son Willie's weekly letter (or fortnightly letter as it more usually is!) for the eleventh or twelfth time, than a hackney carriage pulled up at the door, and who should step out of it but Willie himself!

We have not seen him since just after Christmas, when he went to Oldham a boy. Now, he returns to us a man! It is absurd to imagine that he has grown, since it is only a year to his majority, but he seems taller – or would do, if only he would not slouch so. He wears his hair too long, and has been biting his nails, and his complexion is yellow, like parchment, from the sulphuric air of the north – but otherwise, what a fine figure our son cuts! But how thin – practically consumptive in his appearance! I sent Sarah (my maid) out to buy the ingredients for a beef-steak and kidney pudding, and, leaving *the men* of my family to their manly talk, took myself down to the kitchen to prepare apple dumplings.

AUGUST 5. Eked out our usual leg of mutton with macaronis and cheese, followed by Welsh rarebits and apple fritters, which I am sorry to say Willie hardly touched. Charlie's contribution was a bottle of good port, in which we drank our dear son's health. This toast was the signal for Willie, unbuttoning his waistcoat, to announce that he had 'cut' his first name, and wished henceforth to be known by his second name, Lupin.

I am delighted and honoured that my only son should wish to be known by his mother's maiden name. It is a proud and distinguished name, and one that goes back into the mists of history. The Berkshire Lupins (as my branch is) have graves in Reading and district dating as far back as 1709. There may be earlier Lupins, but they are indecipherable. The Essex Lupins, mainly small-holding stock, may be traced back to the seventeenth century, so I have been told. There have been many outstanding Lupins. Edward Lupin was a member of the Metropolitan Board of Works. Alexander Lupin was at the University of Durham, later to become the general manager of the Mutual Steam Boiler Insurance Company. Several Lupins emigrated to America, where they made their fortunes. Percival Lupin, my great-grandfather, was a respected jobbing printer in Streatham.

Lupin Pooter! So I shall address him with joy – but I shall ever think of him as Willie.

AUGUST 6. Bank Holiday. Lupin not down until a quarter to three. The Bank must have been working him to exhaustion, for him to need so much sleep.

His father asked if he meant to go back by the 5.30 train – Charlie really is the most unobservant of men! He has been up to our boy's room often enough: has he not noticed his belongings – or does he suppose that Lupin has brought his portmanteau, his carpet bag, his hat box, his travelling card table, his umbrella, his dressing case, his Newmarket coat, his banjo, his collection of comic songs, his hammock, all his books and periodicals, and back numbers of *Moonshine*, and four pairs of boots, merely to spend the weekend with us? Poor Charlie was finally made to comprehend what I have known all along: that Lupin and Throstle & Epps' Linen Bank have parted 'brass rags.' Not before time: it is a third-rate, dowdy, provincial place from all I gather, and Lupin's virtues, which are many, were wasted upon the common persons with whom he was forced to rub shoulders. Now, he is at liberty to do what Charlie should have advised him to do in the first place – namely, to offer his services to one of the Lombard

Street banks, such as Lloyds Barnetts & Bosanquets, or the London & County Banking Co Ltd, and to live at home, where he belongs.

AUGUST 7. It is good to have Lupin about the house, so merry and bright! This morning, in marked contrast to yesterday, he was up and about before seven, and singing at the top of his voice that 'Spoofer was his name and what a swell was he.' Fortunately, our neighbour, Mrs Ledgard, has gone to Llandudno for the month, letting her house to some colonial gentlemen – from Canada, we believe. They are very noisy, much given to slamming doors at all hours. Doubtless Mrs Ledgard selected her sub-tenants for that very quality.

For our own part, we shall be spending our usual week, commencing on Monday, at what it pleases

Pretending to twirl his moustaches

75

Charlie to call 'good old' Broadstairs. I should have liked to have gone to Brighton for a change, particularly now that Lupin will be with us; but I know what Charlie would have said: 'And have my "best girl" being "given the eye" by "the mashers"? No jolly old thank you!' – this with a hand on his hip and the other pretending to twirl his moustaches. He says this every time I mention Brighton. He has said it nine times in as many years.

AUGUST 8. The pink Garibaldi and blue-serge skirt, which I have had made for Broadstairs, arrived by parcel post from Annie Fullers (now Mrs James, of Sutton). I burned the wrapping paper, so that Charlie shan't know that I am no longer buying my holiday things of Miss Jibbons, who happens to be acquainted with his cousin Beatrice in Clapham. Enclosed with Annie's bill was a letter bringing good news. The proprietors of 'Fancy Joys' have made a far more generous offer for Mr James' Bronchial Cigarillos manufactory than he was allowing himself to hope for; he will get a good half of his capital back, and is even now making overtures to his former partners in the coal business. Meanwhile, Annie's dressmaking enterprise goes from strength to strength – she is having to refuse lucrative commissions, so busy is she. My dear friend writes that another visit from me is 'long overdue.' I reply by return of post that it is Annie's turn to stay with us for a few days.

AUGUST 13. To Broadstairs. Not our usual rooms, as Charlie left it too late to secure them, but clean apartments near the station. 'Halloh! Quite the home from home!' observed Lupin, as a passing train rattled the windows. Our son has become something of a wit – I don't know where he gets it from.

AUGUST 14. Last night Lupin came in very late from a concert at the Assembly Rooms, full of the new comic songs – 'And he "wunk" the other eye' and 'All very fine and large.' I thought they were highly amusing, but

Last night Lupin came in very late

Charlie, who seems to resent the boy enjoying himself, began grumbling and picking fault. I had to remind him – and myself – that he was young himself once. Charlie said: 'That's all very well, but he gave me to understand last night that he meant to sit up and read, not go gadding off to some third-rate entertainment.' I said: 'You cannot have your cake and eat it. The boy went out in disgust because you made such a song and dance about his choice of reading matter.' Lupin has been engrossed in a yellow-back shocker, *The Witness From The Grave*. Ordinarily, I could not approve of it myself, either, but after all, we are at the seaside.

AUGUST 15. By train to Margate, where the first person we met was Mr Gowing. Charlie seemed surprised. I was not. My only surprise was not to find Mr Cummings there also. That omission, however, is soon to be remedied. 'You know the Cummings' are here too?' said Mr Gowing. I said, through gritted teeth: 'O, that will be delightful! We must have some evenings together and have games!'

If we went to the North Pole, we should bump into Mr Cummings and Mr Gowing, and end up playing 'Consequences.'

AUGUST 16. Charlie has already remarked on the full-ness of the sleeves of my new Garibaldi, made for me by Annie Fullers (now Mrs James, of Sutton) – or Miss Jibbons, as he imagines. Today, as we walked down the Parade, I fancied I heard an errand-boy call: 'What price balloons!'

AUGUST 17. Had a word with Mrs Womming, our land-lady, about the meat she is serving us. There is not enough of it, and what there is, is all gristle. She imme-

I fancied I heard an errand-boy call 'What price balloons!'

diately got up on her 'high horse,' tossing her head and saying 'she'ad only taken us in to oblige,' and so on. She then said: '*And* whilst we're on the subjeck, p'raps you'll'ave a word with young Mr Pooter about 'is whistling, as it annoys my other guests, which is *regulars*.' Next year it shall be Brighton or nowhere.

AUGUST 18. Mr Gowing and Mr Cummings walked over to arrange an evening at Margate, leaving Mrs Cummings behind to twiddle her thumbs at their lodgings. I do not know how she puts up with it. Her husband is at our house practically every night of the week – he dines with us – he carries on as if he were a bachelor – and Mrs Cummings never seems to mind. Perhaps she is as glad to see so little of him as we see much. But one would imagine that even the most undemanding wife would require a little attention from her husband during their holiday.

Mr Gowing and Mr Cummings took Lupin off to play billiards, much to Charlie's disgust. He disapproves of the game (but would approve of it soon enough, if Mr Perkupp invited him to a game).

AUGUST 19. Had to lecture Charlie for treating Lupin as if he were a mere child. Like the contrary creature he is sometimes, he at once went the other way and gave the boy a cigar – as if our son didn't already smoke enough, without encouragement.

Taking a turn on the Parade this afternoon, I saw ever such a tall and straight-backed figure ahead of us, wearing what I believe is the blazer of one of the cavalry regiments. I am almost positive it was Mr Darwitts, but Charlie would dawdle so, we never caught up with him.

AUGUST 20. The last day of our holiday. Bought a Gossware windmill with the Broadstairs coat of arms. Then by train to Margate, to play silly games at the Cummings' and Mr Gowing's lodgings. Bought a Gossware clog with the Margate coat of arms, near the station. Mr Gowing introduced us to a game called 'Cutlets,' in which we all had to sit on one another's laps (he thought I was going to sit on his!). As so often when Mr Gowing is the instigator, we ended up sprawled on the floor, and I banged my head on the fender. When we get home I shall make Charlie write to the Excelsior Fire, Flood & Accident Assurance Co, enquiring as to the premium for insurance against injury caused by parlour games.

Annie Fullers (now Mrs James) comes up from Sutton, bringing one of the new smock-frocks. Mrs Ledgard takes a quiet boarding-house in Llandudno. Charlie confesses to keeping a diary, and insists upon reading from it. My birthday. A commotion over some missing pages. Lupin makes a momentous announcement.

7

AUGUST 21. Back home. House fusty and beds not aired. Have my suspicions that Sarah (my maid) has been spending most of her time at her sister's in The Borough. Why else would a new jar of piccalilli remain untouched (she is very partial to piccalilli)? The half pound of butter I left is finished, but she would have taken that over to The Borough.

Went out into the garden and picked up an 'Opera Puffs' cigarette packet by the wall. I thought it must have been tossed there by Mrs Ledgard's Canadians, but Sarah said: 'No, mum, that lot'ad gone, and this was a new lot, from Australia, being as'ow Mrs Ledgard was staying on at Llandudno for the extra month.'

AUGUST 25. Annie Fullers (now Mrs James) arrived for a few days, from Sutton. She fetched up with her a blue smock-frock which she had run up, from her own design, for a Mrs Rathbone, of Cheam, who is just about my size. It appears that Mr Rathbone has set his face against the smocking rage and will not tolerate his wife wearing the dress. Annie is prepared to do any alterations that may be necessary, and let me have it for two-thirds of the original price.

Mr James' negotiations with his former partners in the coal business have come to naught, and he is now interesting himself in a new concern, which is setting out to manufacture buffalo-meat dog biscuits.

AUGUST 26. To church with Annie. The Vicar shook

hands with her most warmly, and made some complimentary remarks about Sutton. Perhaps he will be less perfunctory with *his own parishioners* in future.

In the afternoon, found Charlie roaming up and down his flowerbeds in an agitated manner, and peering intently at the earth. He was in a rage, accusing the men next door of throwing a firecracker at his tall hat, and swearing that he would find the evidence. Granted that Mrs Ledgard's Australians are even noisier than her Canadians (she must get them from an agency), I do occasionally sense that Charlie suffers from persecution mania. It shows in his diary.

AUGUST 27. With Annie Fullers (now Mrs James, of Sutton) to Peter Robinson, Dickins & Jones and other emporia, to buy stuffs for her dressmaking enterprise. Annie tells me that she is now so well-established that she only has to supervise the work, having set it for others to do, and is able to pass her afternoons with the ladies of fashion who have taken her up. At Dalby & Dalby's in Regent Street, where we bought crêpe for trimming, I was embarrassed to hear Annie inform the floorwalker that 'she was Trade, and would he deduct the usual discount.' He did so without demur. How my arms ached by the time we got back to 'The Laurels,' Annie being adamant that she wanted to carry most of her packages with her.

In the evening I prepared an agreeable cold collation. Mr Gowing came over; and Lupin, for once, stayed in with us, to be sociable to our guest. Annie introduced us to a new game of cards, called 'Muggings,' which I thoroughly enjoyed; but Lupin (to Charlie's annoyance) became very hoity-toity and sarcastic about it, saying: 'Pardon me, this sort of thing is too fast for me' and the like. When we were alone, Annie confided: 'I only suggested "Muggings" because I thought it was "the Holloway thing to do." In Sutton, we play contract whist.'

AUGUST 29. Despite his many influential acquaintance-

My husband read interminably from his diary

ships in the City, Charlie is having difficulty in finding a place for our son. Whilst Annie Fullers (now Mrs James) was packing for her return to Sutton, with the help of Sarah (my maid), he drew me aside and asked 'whether Mrs James, if I approached her, would have a word with Mr James about finding something for the boy?' (He knows that Mr James has sold out of 'Cigar de Ozone' Bronchial Cigarillos, but believes him to have made 'a killing'.) I replied: 'I would never presume on my deep friendship with Annie, to ask such a favour. Besides, all Mr James' business affairs are in the direction of Croydon. It would mean Lupin leaving home again.' Charlie sighed: 'He may as well, for all that we see of him,' and sat down to write to Smethurst & Nephews in Cannon Row, who might have something.

Before Annie left, I showed off my new smock-frock,

which fits almost perfectly. Charlie is at one with Mr Rathbone on the smocking rage.

SEPTEMBER 8. Good news. Mrs Ledgard, so Sarah (my maid) learns, will *not* be returning to Brickfield Terrace, except to supervise the removal of her belongings, as she has taken a fancy to Llandudno, where she proposes to establish a quiet boarding-house. The Australians will be gone by the end of the month, when we may look forward to having orthodox neighbours again. *Lady Cartmell's Vade Mecum For The Bijou Household*, having now dealt with 'Visiting', advises that 'it will be etiquette for the mistress of a house in a new locality, to wait until the *established inhabitants* of the neighbourhood call upon her.' I fancy I have now resided long enough in Brickfield Terrace to fall into that category.

SEPTEMBER 22. Spent another quiet evening with Charlie – Lupin is not much at home, as he has to 'catch up on London life,' as he puts it. I wish he would tell us where he goes.

After reading his *Exchange and Mart* for an hour, Charlie suddenly said: 'So you do not think a man should have a hobby?' – as if our disagreement over Belgian hare rabbits had taken place two minutes ago, instead of two months ago.

I said: 'A man *should* have a hobby, Charles, but one that befits his station in life. You tell me that Mr Spotch, at the office, who is no more than your equal, makes a hobby of cultivating greenhouse ferns. Mr Spotch does *not* breed rabbits, nor keep racing pigeons.'

After digesting this, Charlie said: 'Then perhaps you will be kind enough to tell me, what hobby would be suitable?'

I said, with a straight face: 'Why, you could do worse than to keep a diary!'

Charles stared at me, then roared with laughter, then slapped his knee and cried: 'Carrie, the time has come for your naughty husband to confess his secret! *I have been keeping a diary this many a long month!'*

He then bounded from the parlour, to return a moment later, having recovered his scribbling diary from its hiding place behind our uniform set of 'Great Writers' in the drawing room bookcase. For the rest of the evening, until Lupin came in soon after midnight, my husband read interminably from his diary, exorcising only those passages critical towards his wife.

SEPTEMBER 30. After cold Sunday supper, Charlie produced his diary (he now keeps it in the cabinet) and regaled me with his effusions for the week. I fear this is likely to be a feature of our Sundays from now on.

OCTOBER 7. The Vicar's sermon this evening was 35 minutes. Charlie's diary reading took 40 minutes. Hard put to keep my eyes open during the former ordeal, and failed utterly to do so during the latter.

OCTOBER 19. My birthday. Eleven cards (one more than last year, Lupin's father being at hand to remind him of his filial obligations). Charlie gave me the dear little brooch I had pointed out to him in Zimmerman Bros' window last week, Lupin an amusing novelty sovereign case in which, at the touch of a spring, the inserted coin appears to vanish. We had a bottle of champagne, shared with Mr Cummings, Mr Gowing, and some friends of Lupin's – one Edgar Shanks, Arthur Bonilard (if I heard correctly) and Stanley Chelmsley, who came to carry our son off to *Lipman's Folly Burlesques* at the Britannia, Hoxton. Young Mr Chelmsley's father is standing treat, as he has the advertising contract for the safety curtain, and can get free tickets (unlike Mr Merton, of 'Lockanbar' fame!) – one may take it, then, that the entertainment has the stamp of Mr Chelmsley, Senr's, approval.

OCTOBER 20. Not a mention of his wife's birthday in Charles' diary yesterday. He chose instead to devote the whole page to some imagined slight by one of his office whippersnappers.

OCTOBER 21. Usual Sunday diary reading. Upon Charlie drawing breath as he reached 'October 19th,' I interjected: 'My wonderful birthday!' The poor chap, he was as startled as I have ever seen him. He stared wildly at the page, and then commenced an extemporised recitation of what I was to imagine was an exhaustive eulogy to my birthday: 'A red letter day in our house, my dear little wifey's birthday' &c &c &c. I made him stammer through a whole 'page' of it. How I inwardly roared!

OCTOBER 29. Upon going into the kitchen, found my charwoman, Mrs Birrell, on the verge of ripping half the pages out of the latest weekly part of *Lady Cartmell's Vade Mecum For The Bijou Household*, to wrap up some scraps she was taking home. As soon as the last number is out, I shall ask Charlie to have my *Lady Cartmell* bound up.

OCTOBER 30. The house in an uproar, because Charlie has opened his diary, only to find the last five or six weeks torn out. He at once suspected me. I should like to know why: if he believes me enraptured by his diary readings, why should I frustrate him by destroying his scribblings? – yet if he believes me bored to suffocation by them, why would he torment me by persisting with them? I told him it was his own fault for leaving his wretched diary lying about. He waved his arms in a grandiose manner, and knocked over a vase given to me for our wedding by Mrs Burtsett, of Dalston. I let him believe I was very upset; in truth, I never liked Mrs Burtsett or her vase, and it is a relief to see the back of it.

NOVEMBER 3. Momentous and disturbing news. Out of the blue, Lupin announces himself *engaged to be married* – to a Miss Daisy Mutlar, who belongs to the set he has been going about with. The poor boy is but twenty summers. We have not met Miss Mutlar, and he has never spoken of her before. She sounds very 'fast' to me. I had better say no more on the subject for the present.

We learn a little of Miss Daisy Mutlar, and are later introduced, when some earlier misapprehensions are corrected. Lupin finds a berth. The Misses Tipper inspect the house next door, but find it wanting. Charles shows his mettle with the charwoman. We plan a grand party in honour of Miss Mutlar.

8

NOVEMBER 5. Miss Daisy Mutlar resides in Upper Holloway, at 'Avoncrest,' No. 17, Atha Grove, with her parents and brother. They have two servants living-in – cook-general and maid. I chanced to pass along Atha Grove on my afternoon walk yesterday, and could not help but notice the house; it is a double-fronted residence with a porch, and claret glass surrounds to the bay windows, with engraved corner sunbursts.

Miss Mutlar's father is Mutlar, Williams and Watts. They sound a highly respected firm, although Charlie has not heard of them.

Miss Mutlar is somewhat older than Lupin, although he will not say by how many summers. She is neither tall nor short – of the medium height, I gather. She occupies herself with charitable works, arranging recitals and lectures for tramps and other unfortunates, at the North London Outcasts' Haven and Day Refuge for the Homeless; and also occasionally assists her widowed aunt, a Mrs Clifford, who manages a select circulating library.

Lupin was introduced to Miss Mutlar by her brother, Mr Frank Mutlar, who is a member of the 'Holloway Comedians', an Amateur Dramatic Club to which Lupin has recently been elected. Mr Mutlar Jnr is with Ballard, Sim & Co, Shipping Agents, St Mary Axe, there being nothing suitable for him at present in the family business. Miss Mutlar herself does *not* indulge in amateur theatricals; but she is an accomplished pianist, and has a better voice than many professional concert singers.

She speaks a little French fluently. Miss Mutlar has not been engaged before, that our son is aware of. That is the sum of our knowledge of Miss Mutlar for the present.

The 'engagement' has not yet been put on a formal footing, Lupin neither having bought a ring, nor asked Mr Mutlar for his daughter's hand. Nor would he be prudent to do so, until he is more confident of his prospects – happily, Mr Perkupp may know of something for him. He is to go down and see about it tomorrow.

It seems only yesterday since I was pushing our little son in his bassinette across Peckham Rye. I do hope Daisy will make him happy. They will take their first rooms nearby, I hope and trust. I have several things laid by – unwanted wedding presents, including superfluous antimacassars, some duplicate jelly and pudding moulds, and most of a tea and breakfast service – that will give them a start. Can she cook? I wonder. This I know, my diary: I shall love her as my own daughter.

NOVEMBER 6. To our relief, Lupin has accepted a position with Messrs Job Cleanands and Co, Stock and Share Brokers. However, his salary is little enough, and I asked Charlie to remind him, at some opportune moment, that two *cannot* live as cheaply as one. Charlie said drily: 'He must have observed that for himself.' I asked my husband sharply, what he meant by that. He replied hastily: 'Only that Lupin "touched" me for half a sovereign on Saturday. Miss Mutlar must have expensive tastes!' I hope she is not leading him on.

Fireworks, in the rain, at the Cummings', this evening. '*A damp squib,*' I remarked to Charlie on the way home. He said without a smile: 'Yes – a complete waste of money.' He can be very dense sometimes.

NOVEMBER 7. Lupin asked me to call on Mrs Mutlar. After consulting with *Lady Cartmell's Vade Mecum For The Bijou Household*, I informed him that it was Mrs Mutlar's place to call on me. Lupin cried: 'O, pooh, mater! Tomkins stood on ceremony, and look at Tomkins

94

now!' As so often now-a-days, I had not an inkling what our son was talking about. Charlie took my part, and the argument would have gone on all night, had I not pointed out that we had no visiting cards left, and that the time to discuss the etiquette of calling was when we had had some more printed. I suggested Messrs Darwitts', the wholesale stationers, specialists in letterheads, feint-rule ledger sheets &c &c, who advertise in *The Globe*, but Charles said coldly that 'I had Darwitts' on the brain, and he would go to Black's, as usual.' Our last 'as usual' for twenty-five visiting cards apiece must have been four years ago.

NOVEMBER 8. Lupin brought his friend Frank Mutlar back from the 'Holloway Comedians' for supper. I wanted to draw Mr Mutlar out about his sister, but Lupin would keep on encouraging him to do skits and 'turns' for our amusement. His imitation of a cross-eyed waiter serving soup was quite funny, but I wished he had not done it with real soup. When I said as much to Sarah (my maid and cook-general), by way of explaining the stains on the cloth, she said, in all seriousness: 'But real it was not, mum, as *you* should know − *it was mock turtle*!' This I found so droll that I repeated it to Charlie. He said: 'Yes, I hope young Master Mutlar hasn't run off with the idea that we can't afford the real thing.'

NOVEMBER 9. Mrs Ledgard's house has stood empty since her Australians left, a month ago. This morning, whom should I see the agent escorting into the house, but the Misses Tipper! Presently they called, and I enter-tained them to breakfast chocolate, the day being cold. They are still mindful to come to Holloway, to be near their brother, if they can find a suitable property; but they did not 'take to' the house next door. It is not so much the proximity of the railway (both ladies are some-what hard of hearing), as the damage done to the paint and varnish − cigar-burns, scuff-marks, and so on − by Mrs Ledgard's Canadians or Australians, or both. I promised to keep my eye open on the Misses Tippers' behalf. It is a shame we cannot have them as neighbours.

NOVEMBER 10. Had to go up four times to awaken Lupin this morning – finally rousing him with a wet face-flannel. He had to run out of the house without his break-fast, in order to catch his 'bus, and so was forced to work all morning with nothing but a halfpenny bun from a coffee shop inside him. But – whilst he grumbles that Messrs Job Cleanands are 'more sharepushers than stockbrokers' – he likes his new berth well enough, and is evidently making a good impression. Talked a good deal about Daisy Mutlar at tea, until Charlie said: 'Don't your organ play another tune?' – an expression he has picked up from Lupin, for all that he professes to find the boy's speech incomprehensible!

NOVEMBER 11. Charlie has at last learned what I could have told him all along – that the missing pages from his diary were torn out by Mrs Birrell, the charwoman, to whom newspapers, periodicals, letters, bills, sheet music and even bound volumes are but so much butter paper. I wish his enquiries could have come to a head on a day other than when Mrs Birrell took it into her head to help herself to the 'Lockanbar' whisky – thinking, pro-bably, that we had forgotten it was in the cellar. The woman made a frightening and ugly scene with Sarah (my maid), who had unwisely warned her that 'the Master'ad his suspicions' concerning the lost pages. I was afraid to intervene; Lupin did his best, but lacked the experience to be effectual; and it was Charlie, arriving opportunely, who took command of the situa-tion, and restored order by sending Mrs Birrell about her business. When the need arises, my husband can be as masterful as any ship's captain. Would that Mr Perkupp had been here, to witness those qualities in his servant of which he knows naught!

NOVEMBER 12. On the way home from church (wherein, I

confess to my shame, I indulged myself, all through the sermon, in phantasies of a certain marriage service!), we met, at long last, Miss Daisy Mutlar, accompanied by Lupin and her brother. I hope I was mistaken in my impression that they made as if to cross the road when they saw us coming.

Miss Mutlar is *not* of the medium height. She is what I would call large, being big-boned; as well as a good three inches taller than Lupin, even though not on high heels (she probably would like to wear them but cannot – the rest of her dress, although by no means 'flash,' was not, I thought, subdued enough for a Sunday). She is too old for him – Charlie says she can give him eight years, I say a good ten. Her hair is no stranger to the automatic hair curler.

I contrived to walk alone with Miss Mutlar, ahead of the others. I found her sensible and respectful in conversation, although given to an irritating giggle at the merest pleasantry. This is probably nerves. She was kind enough to admire my hat, and to enquire as to the name of my milliner (the Holloway *Bon Marché,* as it so happens in this instance – I recommended Mme Parkin, whom I patronise occasionally). Taking one thing with another, Miss Mutlar seems a nice young woman, who makes the best of a naturally plain appearance.

NOVEMBER 13. Spent the morning writing invitations, as we have asked Miss Daisy Mutlar and her brother over on Wednesday, to meet a few of our friends. It must be as nice an affair as I can make it.

Earlier, a contrite Mrs Birrell had arrived at the area front door first thing, with a card of press-studs as a peace offering to Sarah (my maid). She begged for a second chance. I said: 'Very well, Mrs Birrell, if Sarah accepts your apology. But you are to understand this. *I* am the mistress of this house, and I *will not* have you using paper indiscriminately. In future, back copies of *The Globe, Jepson's Sunday Newspaper* and the *Exchange and Mart* will be left for your use by the pantry door, and you will use no other, whether it appears to you to be of any use or no.' I was rather proud of that speech, although I wished I had employed an alternative to one of the three 'uses' in my last sentence. I believe that Charlie, had he seen his wife so firmly in command of her household, would have been proud of me too.

NOVEMBER 14. The following have sent word that they take pleasure (or, in some cases, have the honour) of accepting our invitation to a reception at 'The Laurels' tomorrow:

Miss Daisy Mutlar

Mr Perkupp (if able to get away from a previous engagement, in Kensington)

Mr Stillbrook

Mr Nackles

Mr Burwin-Fosselton (of the 'Holloway Comedians')

Mr Frank Mutlar

Mr & Mrs James, of Sutton

Mr & Mrs Cummings

Mr Gowing

Mr Franching, of Peckham

Mr Merton

Mr Sprice-Hogg and the Misses Sprice-Hogg

Messrs Watson, Chelmsley, Shanks, Bonnington (*not* Bonilard!) and Shacker, also of the 'Holloway Comedians' accepted orally, with the message (conveyed by Lupin): 'Good biz! Lead us to it!'

The following greatly regretted their inability to attend, much though they would have wished to have given themselves the pleasure:

Mr Brack (of Perkupp & Co – previous engagement)

Mr Fallowes (do   –   do   )

Mr & Mrs Treane (have Mrs Treane's mother staying with them; they would bring her over, but she has to take drops hourly, and would not wish to be a nuisance)

The Misses Tipper (night air does not suit them)

Mr Darwitts (annual dinner of Master Stationers' Coy)

NB: On the advice of Mr Frank Mutlar that his parents live quietly, and do not get out into society, we did not invite Mr and Mrs Mutlar, as we most certainly should otherwise have done – notwithstanding Lupin's tasteless contention that 'old Mutlar is a stick-in-the-mud who would be more at home at a funeral tea – his own!'

Preparations for the reception. Charlie chooses an unfortunate moment to make one of his jokes. An unexpected call by Mrs Shrike, of Bow. Our momentous party. All the guests turn up, including Mr Perkupp, who delicately handles a mishap with a jam puff.

9

NOVEMBER 15. Would that Mrs Ledgard were still here, to observe the procession of cabs, dog-carts, and Mr Perkupp's carriage, that will be drawing up outside 'The Laurels' this evening!

Much, in the meanwhile, to be done, to complement the preparations I have already made for our reception. Spent yesterday making ladies' fingers, saucer-cakes, cocoa-nut buns, jam puffs and jellies. Unfortunately used one of the moulds I had got down from the attic for Lupin and Daisy when they set up home, but which Mrs Birrell has failed to scrub out. Valuable time was lost in picking cinder fragments out of a damson jelly. I had a mind to make an Indian Trifle as a centrepiece, but when I looked for the recipe, which I know I copied out of *Lady Cartmell's Vade Mecum For The Bijou Household* and tucked behind the mantelpiece clock, it was nowhere to be found. Mrs Birrell has learned her lesson, I know; I was forced, therefore, to the conclusion that Charlie has used it as a spill to light his pipe.

I asked him what he knew about the disappearance of my recipe for Indian Trifle. Charlie said, with a chuckle: 'O, my dear Carrie, this is no time to concern yourself with *trifles*!' I drew myself up to my full height and said: 'Charles Pooter, I am very busy with the preparations for our party. Indeed, I am distraught, from the effort of making everything just so, in case your precious Mr Perkupp should *deign* to drop in after visiting his fine friends in Kensington.' Charlie said: 'That is unfair, Caroline. You were the one who *would* invite Mr

Perkupp.' I said: 'You were the one who said he was too grand for us, and that is why I am slaving to make our home look like a palace.' Charlie said: 'It has always been a palace to me, Carrie.' The compliment came just in time, for I chanced to be holding a jug of blanc-mange mixture, of a size approximating to his hat.

The entire evening was spent in re-arranging our pictures and bric-à-brac, and re-arranging them again, hanging muslin over the folding doors &c &c. It was midnight before I sat down. Charlie was preoccupied in nursing his fingers, which he had carelessly trapped whilst taking the drawing room door off its hinges; he hardly noticed my improvements. I said, with unwonted sarcasm: 'Now we need not be ashamed in front of Mr Perkupp, should he honour us by coming.' I am afraid the occasion has put us both a little on edge, and out of humour.

Today, in the morning, glazed a ham and prepared the other cold cuts; made sandwiches; cut the stand pie; and arranged a silver dish of filberts. No luncheon, except for a slice off the cold beef and a few pickles. In the afternoon, arranged my sideboard and side-tables. It took an age. As a finishing touch, placed Liberty silk bows around the corners of our tinted photographs, at the same time putting Aunt Rhoda's portrait away in a cupboard, as the enlargement unfortunately exaggerates a very slight squint. Took one last look around – everything very pretty – and was just about to go upstairs and change, when in came Sarah (my maid) with the announcement: 'Mrs Shrike 'as come, mum.'

Some mistresses are capable of sending word to callers that 'they are not at home.' I am not. A falsehood is a falsehood, whatever convention may say, and whatever be the inconvenience the truth may cause. Besides, Mrs Shrike, of Bow, was already in the room. I shook hands and enquired if she was feeling faint again, on account of her weak blood. She, happily, was not. Mrs Shrike, as before, had intended to visit her brother in Coppernail Terrace, but on this occasion he was out –

seemingly he cannot have received the postcard she sent this morning. Rather than waste the 'bus fare, then, Mrs Shrike determined to call at 'The Laurels.'

I asked Sarah to bring in tea; but Mrs Shrike, with an eye to my sideboard, said: 'Bless you, Mrs Pooter, there's already enough there to feed a regiment! Now a buffet *is* a notion, because one doesn't have to go running in and out making more. As for a beverage, a drop of what you gave me last time would go down very nicely.'

Mrs Shrike has an excellent appetite, despite her weak blood, and did full justice to the cold cuts and the stand pie. I prayed that she would not cut into the glazed ham. My prayers were answered: she only picked off a little of the glaze, and declared it too rich for her constitution. An attack upon the sweetmeats was accompanied by a third glass of port wine; after which Mrs Shrike, avowing that 'she had such a terrible thirst, what with walking up that hill and down again,' disposed of three-quarters of a siphon of soda water. The conversation turned mainly on Mrs Shrike's health (she is improved, but will never be a well woman), and upon her brother, a Mr Hadow, who has a window-cleaning concern in a very large way. I made no mention of our impending party, for fear that Mrs Shrike would take offence at not having been invited; and so she made no effort to hasten her departure, and would doubtless have still been sitting there when the first guests arrived, had not Sarah entered to say that Mr Peters (the waiter we have hired, at Lupin's insistence) had arrived, and wanted a word 'most perticklar.'

Mrs Shrike having taken her leave, I turned the glazed ham and did what else I could to repair the depredations to my sideboard, then went down to receive Mr Peters. He was not in the house; it was a ruse on Sarah's part to get rid of Mrs Shrike, as she had taken it upon herself to think that 'it must be 'igh time you was getting changed, mum.' I said, with *Lady Cartmell*: 'Sarah, a guest's *sixth sense* will inform her when she is overstaying her welcome; if it does not, and good breeding fails to come

Miss Mutlar wore a dress of pillar-box red sateen

to her aid, then the experienced hostess will be capable, by the gentlest and most fleeting of signals, of indicating that the visit has become protracted.' Nevertheless, I gave Sarah a sixpence from my housekeeping purse, and got upstairs precisely at the same time as Charlie, who had come home early. He said: 'Really, Carrie, it's too bad. I had thought to find you ready – now we shall be tripping over one another's feet.' I thought of several rejoinders, but said nothing.

Later: The reception has been almost an unqualified success. I wore my 'Mansion House Ball' dress, and was complimented upon it, not only by Charlie, and its authoress, Annie Fullers (now Mrs James, of Sutton), but also by Miss Mutlar, and one of the Sprice-Hogg girls. Miss Mutlar wore a dress of pillar-box red sateen, which even Annie declared was cut too low, and without a shred of lace to cover her shoulders, which are very large, and freckled. All the guests came who were invited (young Mr Chelmsley, indeed, arrived with two young persons who were not invited, whom he said were his distant cousins; all I can say is that they did not behave distantly enough towards him in my drawing room); not forgetting Mr Perkupp, who came very late, in the middle of a game, and was stand-offish. He required nothing but a glass of soda water; unfortunately, following upon Mrs Shrike's attention to the siphon this afternoon, we had run out of it altogether. He would take nothing else, but said he was 'most pleased to see us in our own home,' as I think he was, or he would not have come. There cannot be many clerks in the City, whose principals would bother to cross London, just to drink their health in soda water (had there been any to drink); it shows how my husband is regarded.

Charlie took Mr Perkupp to his carriage. As they went out I saw that Mr Perkupp had stepped on an open jam puff that must have dropped from somebody's plate. The encumbrance cannot have escaped his notice, his dress boots having thin soles; but neither by word nor gesture did he intimate his awareness of treading cherry jam down the stairs. Whatever his deficiencies as a man of commerce, Mr Perkupp is a gentleman.

Except for the slight awkwardness occasioned by Mr Perkupp's visit, and the silliness of the Sprice-Hogg girls, who were forever running out of the room with their handkerchieves stuffed into their mouths, it was the most enjoyable formal party we have ever given – the other two being on the occasions of our tin and china weddings. We had games, and songs (Miss Mutlar, at Lupin's request, sang four, one after the other; her voice is not good), and recitations. I sang 'The Garden of Sleep'; whilst Mr James, of Sutton, much to the surprise of his friends, recited 'A Sailor's Apology For Bowlegs' by Thomas Hood. Charlie refuses either to sing or to recite in company; more's the pity, since he has a good, if thin, light baritone voice. However, directly Mr Perkupp

had left, he did make so bold as to dance with me —
taking care not to trip this time, for all that he had
knocked back two glasses of port 'in two-four time,' as
Lupin put it. As we waltzed, my dear old Charlie whispered some nonsense in my ear about it 'being like the
old days.' I laughed: 'What a spooney old thing you are!'
and squeezed his hand — quite forgetting that he had
trapped it in the door earlier. 'Trodden on the cat, guv?'
enquired Lupin as he danced by with Miss Mutlar. She
was allowing him to hold her far too close for comfort, to
my way of thinking.

We acquire new neighbours, by name Griffin. Charlie refuses point blank to buy one of the smaller 'Wenham Lake' ice safes. We decline an invitation. A mother's premonitions about Lupin and Daisy. They are confirmed.

10

NOVEMBER 16. Charlie up and down all night, and liverish this morning, as always when he has been taking champagne (not to mention port, and goodness knows what else when my back was turned). Should he ever take to drink, as I sometimes fear he might, his sickly constitution may be the salvation of him.

Great excitement this morning, at what sounded like the First Life Guards clattering along the street. Drew back the curtains to see no fewer than *three* pantechnicons outside Mrs Ledgard's former residence – the house has been let at last. Good quality furniture (ebonised drawing room cabinet too big for the house, as they will find), including a 'Wenham Lake' ice safe – I have seen them in Merryweather's. The smaller van yielded a veritable cornucopia of things for a day nursery – hobby-horses, hoops, spinning tops, race games &c &c, without end. Either they have a great many children, or one spoiled one. Sarah (my maid) has found out from the removal men that the family's name is Griffin, from Dalston.

Was so absorbed with the traffic next door that I forgot to call Lupin, who did not put in an appearance until half past eleven, when he looked as yellow as custard. I asked him what on earth they would have to say at the office? He said: 'O, I'll spin them a tale.' He gets this careless attitude from Miss Mutlar's circle. I do not approve of it.

NOVEMBER 17. Saw Mr Griffin come out of the house and

drive off in a pony-trap. He dresses well, with a tall hat, and carries himself as if he were the principal of his own business. No sign of Mrs Griffin.

At breakfast, asked Charlie if he didn't think the *blanc-mange*, left over from our party, a little warm and sour to the taste. He merely grunted. I said: 'I have been wondering about an ice safe. It would be a boon in a hot summer, when I am forever throwing out meat and dairy stuff that has gone on the "turn". The smaller "Wenham Lake" model is not all that expensive; and it would pay for itself in the end.' Charlie said: 'Then when that day comes, we will order one, and let the ice safe settle up.' I expect he will be telling his little 'joke' all around the office. I thought it cruel.

Mr Gowing came round this evening, ostensibly to thank us for the party (everyone else has sent charming letters, except the tribe of 'Holloway Comedians') but in reality to help us eat our supper. The *blanc-mange* being brought in, he cried: 'Hulloh! The remains of Wednesday?' What breeding!

NOVEMBER 18. Invited to the wedding of Miss Bird — a friend of the James', of Sutton — and a Mr Basil Rugge. Charlie voted to decline, since it would mean a present, and we hardly know Miss Bird. I *shall* decline, but for a different reason. Annie is making the trousseau. Without doubt I should be called upon to spend the week before the marriage ceremony down in Sutton, with a mouthful of pins. Lupin very caustic about the institution of marriage. I am beginning to entertain certain suspicions.

At supper, Charlie threatened to walk out of the house, if the *blanc-mange* were ever placed on the table again. I said: 'It has to be eaten up — unless you would like me to bottle it, which is the only means we have of preserving food in this house.' Gave the last of the *blanc-mange* to our cat, Cinders. She refused it.

NOVEMBER 19. Lupin seemed as happy as a lark, as he

departed to spend the day at the Mutlars'. I do not know what to make of it. What with his cynical observations upon the married state, and the significant fact that he did not see Miss Mutlar at all yesterday – a Saturday – not to mention his occasional fits of 'broodiness,' I have been very apprehensive. I remarked to Charlie, by way of 'sounding him out', that one advantage of Lupin's engagement with Daisy was that he seemed happy all day long. Charlie most cordially agreed; which can only mean that the boy has not unburdened himself to him, and that he has no reservations; therefore my misgivings may be groundless. But I remain uneasy in myself.

Charlie and I had a long talk about the wisdom or otherwise of early engagements. I reminded him that we married early ourselves – I was certainly younger than Daisy Mutlar – and that, although his responsibilities may have held him back, and prevented him from 'taking the plunge' and making something of himself, instead of resigning himself to the patronage and whim of Mr Perkupp, we have been on the whole content. Charlie made a pretty little speech about the contribution to happiness of small privations in one's married life. Wisely, he forbore to include our lack of one of the smaller 'Wenham Lake' ice safes among his examples. He is quite a philosopher, when he has a mind to be. At length the subject was exhausted, and we both fell to writing up our diaries, and then read quietly. I am less perturbed than I was; but a mother's fears persist – if fears they be: would I not be more candid to call them a mother's *hopes*?

Later: Lupin entered the house at twelve minutes past nine, with a face that could have come down from a poster for a melodrama. He drank off what was left of a bottle of 'Lockanbar' from the party – a good wineglassful, neat – then threw himself into a chair and smoked moodily.

I pretended to read for an hour; until at last I felt compelled to take the bull by the horns. I said to Lupin, my voice shaking: 'I hope Daisy is well?'

He said: 'You mean Miss Mutlar? I don't know whether she is well or not, but *please never to mention her name again in my presence.*'

His affected airiness of tone all but broke his mother's heart; yet for all that, it was relief that surged into my bosom.

'The Laurels' versus *'The Larches'* – *impending confusion. Lupin turns to the bottle. Evenings with 'Henry Irving'. I make the acquaintance of Mrs Griffin. A Mr Elphinstone is my unwitting ally.*

11

NOVEMBER 20. Turning out yesterday's *Jepson's Sunday Newspaper*, my eye fell upon a sad little announcement to the effect that the marriage that had been arranged between Miss So-and-so and Mr Such-and-such, would not now take place. What a blessing, the 'engagement' never having been official, that the name of *Pooter* shall not figure in such an announcement, for all to see, in the columns of the *City Press*!

Noticed Mr Putley, the decorator, painting a sign on next door's fanlight. Going out to post a letter to Mother a few minutes later, saw that where Mrs Ledgard had only a number – No. 14 – the Griffins have elected to call their house 'The Larches.' It is very vexing. 'The Larches' may so easily be confused with 'The Laurels,' by anyone who comes out without the precise address written down. Then there is the post – we have had trouble enough with wrong deliveries already. If they must have a name, why not 'Fairlawn' or 'Two Chimneys,' for example? 'The Larches' is preposterous. There is not a larch in the street.

NOVEMBER 21. Fear that Lupin may be seeking solace in drink – potentially, a family weakness. We have seen next to nothing of him, but tonight he put in an appearance for a few minutes, when he asked his father for a little brandy. Told that there was none in the house, he stormed out, to who knows what alehouse or gin palace. I said to Charlie: 'If the boy *must* turn to the bottle at such a time, better he drink with his father, with whom he may talk things over man to man, than with low company in a whisky cabin.' Charlie said: 'Lupin has no head for spirits.' I said: 'No more have you, but that has never held you back from drinking them.'

NOVEMBER 22. I am so heartily sick of the sound of Miss Daisy Mutlar's name, in one endless roundelay of a discussion after another with Charlie, that I was almost pleased to see Mr Cummings and Mr Gowing this evening. Lupin, to my surprise and pleasure, also came in, bringing his friend Mr Burwin-Fosselton, of the 'Holloway Comedians.' Of the five known breakages resulting from our party the other night – two smashed wine glasses, an antimacassar stud ripped off the ottoman, a broken fruit plate, and a cracked occasional table – all were perpetrated by 'Holloway Comedians,' not one of whom has sent his apology (much less his thanks for the evening). Mr Burwin-Fosselton, as he insists upon being styled (a mere 'Fosselton' will not do for him) was responsible for the damage to the table, by leaning heavily upon it whilst doing an imitation of Mr Henry Irving, whom he is said to resemble, and which Lupin had brought him in to repeat. For myself, I believe he more nearly resembles the young man in the 'Before Use' portion of the advertisement for Dr Sibson's 'Lakgoh' Debility Pills; but I will put up with any amount of his nonsense, if it will only take my poor Lupin out of himself.

NOVEMBER 23. Have changed my laundress, and now wish I hadn't. The old one fetched all my whites back yellow, but at least she fetched them back. If the present one loses any more of Charlie's socks and collars, he will have to go down to the office bare-footed in his boots, and wearing a muffler.

More Irving imitations from Mr Burwin-Fosselton, who on this occasion brought his make-up. Mr Gowing brought a friend of his, a Mr Padge, a man of little conversation. Mr Cummings, mercifully, brought only himself. Sooner or later, I shall have to make it plain that the parlour of 'The Laurels' is not to be confused with the pit of the Elephant & Castle Theatre.

NOVEMBER 24. Called on Mrs Griffin at 'The Larches.' I was kept waiting in the hall rather longer than is customary, but was received pleasantly enough. The house is still at 'sixes and sevens,' but looks as if it will be very comfortable when everything is in its proper place. Thinking to pay a compliment, I said as much to Mrs Griffin.

Mrs Griffin said, after a short silence: 'Everything *is* in its proper place, Mrs Pooter, or you should not have found me at home.'

It is the ebonised drawing room cabinet that is partly the trouble. It makes her drawing room look like the Ladies' Coffee Room at the Midland Grand Hotel at King's Cross. But, as Mrs Griffin's guest, it was not for me to say so. Another disturbing element is the air of general untidiness occasioned by giving children free rein of the drawing room – toys visible under cushions, where they had been hastily concealed; and a *Chatterbox* annual with its cover hanging off, wedged into a set of the *Waverley Novels*. Whilst I was talking to Mrs Griffin, there was a scuffling outside the door, which presently burst open, and a number of boys fell into the room, and then retired, chortling and hooting. I do not know how many: I asked Mrs Griffin how many children she had, but she only said: 'Too many.' Thereafter, during the whole of my visit, they ran up and down the stairs unchecked, what time the door of the drawing room stood wide open, with a draught blowing in.

Presently I said to Mrs Griffin: 'By-the-by, I see that you have called your house "The Larches." Was there any particular reason for that choice of name?'

Mrs Griffin said: 'Does one have to have a *particular* reason?'

I said: 'By no means – but there are no larches in Brickfield Terrace.'

She said: 'There are no laurels either.'

I explained that there had been two laurel bushes in our front garden, until workmen, looking for a gas leak, had dug them up, and never replaced them.

I said: 'We do have a mind to plant more laurels.'

Mrs Griffin said: 'We have a mind to plant larches.'

I left the matter there, being too polite to remind my neighbour that as the *senior* of our two families in terms of residence in Brickfield Terrace, we were entitled to deference from *newcomers* in the matter of house-names. Let her wait until one of Mr Griffin's important friends presents himself at the wrong house!

Mrs Griffin, noticing the fob watch which Charlie gave me for our first married Christmas, enquired, 'was her clock fast, as it sometimes gained?' This I took as a signal to leave. Mrs Griffin did not offer me tea; and I was all but knocked down by a horde of boys as I went out.

The Irving imitations continue their 'unprecedented run,' although Mr Burwin-Fosselton will have noticed that 'Mr Wood' was in the 'house' this evening – i.e., he had to play to a diminished audience. Lupin was elsewhere; Mr Cummings came, but not Mr Gowing. To Charlie's exasperation, Mr Gowing's friend Mr Padge came by himself. I murmured: 'Does he possess a ticket, or is he a friend of the manager?' To my embarrassment, Mr Padge overheard the aside; but he only beamed, and said: 'That's right.' To help things along, the conversation becoming wearisome, I did what I considered to be quite a good impersonation of Ellen Terry, inviting Mr Burwin-Fosselton to play opposite me in a 'spoof' improvisation of *The Bells*. He declined haughtily, saying that 'farce was *not* within his *repertoire*.' I fancy that this was Mr Burwin-Fosselton's 'last and positively final appearance' so far as the audience at 'The Laurels' is concerned.

NOVEMBER 25. A Mr Elphinstone called. I thought he had come looking for the Irving imitations – a friend of Mr Padge, perhaps – but no; he had mistaken 'The Laurels' for 'The Larches.' My case is made.

Mrs Griffin makes an impertinent suggestion. Charlie talks grandly about his diary. The Griffin boys are tiresome. I buy some 'Darwitts' 'Xmas cards, but have to put them away. Lupin's unfortunate engagement is on again.

12

DECEMBER 4. Mrs Griffin returned my call of a few days ago. I gave Sarah (my maid) a significant nod, to indicate my desire for there to be no cutting of corners in the matter of serving tea. The girl excelled herself to the point of imbecility, bringing in every bun and biscuit in the house, as well as a pippin flan from Borset's, and sufficient salmon-paste sandwiches for a Sunday School treat. Mrs Shrike, of Bow, would have been in her element. Mrs. Griffin had half a cup of tea, and crumbled a ratafia on a plate, but did not eat it, and otherwise touched nothing.

Mrs Griffin said, after we had discussed the intolerable noise made by shunting trains lately: 'By-the-by, Mrs Pooter, I noticed that the card you sent in, when you were good enough to call, doesn't bear your address.'

That is so. *Lady Cartmell's Vade Mecum For the Bijou Household* decrees that either form is correct — with, or without, the address. Charlie and I talked it over, and decided upon the name only. Should we ever remove from this house (*which I hope we shall!*), our cards would not have to be altered in pen and ink or thrown away; moreover, with the name only, it is a shilling per twenty-five cheaper.

I bowed, to acknowledge the accuracy of the observation.

Mrs Griffin said: 'You will have noticed that our cards have the address — "The Larches," Brickfield Terrace, Holloway, N.'

Scrutinising Mrs Griffin's card between thumb and

index finger, I said: 'Yes. They are very nicely done.'

Mrs Griffin said: 'Upon reflection, I think you are right, Mrs Pooter, as to possible confusion arising out of the similarity between the names of our houses.'

I said: 'I believe so, Mrs Griffin. Only yesterday, a quantity of coals was nearly poured down our coal-hole in mistake for yours; and recently a Mr Elphinstone came to our door, mistaking "The Laurels" for "The Larches." '

Mrs Griffin said: 'I suggest that, before the situation becomes intolerable, one or other of us should give way.'

At this, I held my tongue. 'One or *other*' of us indeed!

Mrs Griffin said: 'We should gladly be the ones to think of another name, if only we hadn't put ourselves to the expense of having our cards printed already, with our address in the corner. I venture to wonder, Mrs Pooter, since *your* address doesn't appear on your visiting cards. . . .'

I was ready for her little ploy. I said: 'Ah! But Mrs Griffin! Think of our having to throw away the embossing die for our stationery – a costly business. Besides, we have already had our Christmas calendars printed.' This last was a white lie – we do not send out Christmas calendars. Nonetheless, it had the desired effect, and there the matter rests.

DECEMBER 18. With a thousand and one things to be done in time for Christmas, have had no time to keep up this diary. Would that Charlie had had no time to keep up his. Since the affair of the missing pages, there have been no more readings aloud. Yesterday, however, Charlie, carrying his scribbling diary under his arm, entered the parlour in a self-important manner, and, placing it upon my torchère for want of a lectern, proceeded to read from it, as if he were Charles Dickens himself. I walked out of the room for fear of bursting out laughing, so comical were his gesticulations.

This morning he broached the subject at breakfast, voicing his disappointment at what he takes to be my lack of interest (he does not know that I read each entry almost before the ink is dry), and voicing his hopes of having his diary published one day, like Evelyn and Pepys! This time I *did* burst out laughing, as did Lupin, who retorted cruelly that the volume 'might get a fair price from a butterman.'

None of which discouraged Charlie from copying out a list of publishing houses from the *Pegg's Commercial & Shipping Almanack*, which he has borrowed from the office. I shall copy out the list myself before he returns it.

DECEMBER 19. Hearing a commotion in the back, looked out and saw the Griffin boys walking along the garden wall, holding raspberry canes, as if they were tightrope-walkers in a circus. One of them fell into our flower bed, but at once scrambled back. I do not know how many of them there were: they would not remain still enough to be counted. Later, the day being clement for this time of year, I took a walk down the garden, where I encountered Mrs Griffin, walking down hers. We bowed. I said: 'By-the-by, Mrs Griffin, our party wall is not as safe as it might be, as the pointing is crumbled. Some of your children were playing on it earlier, and I wish they would not.' Mrs Griffin said: 'Not some – *all*.' I do not understand that woman.

DECEMBER 20. Looking at Christmas cards in the Fancy Bazaar, I found a whole counter devoted to the 'Darwitts'' range of snow scenes, most reasonably priced. I thought I had better take two dozen, our having made so many new friends this year. As I might have known, when Charlie came home, he proved to have taken it into his head to buy the Christmas cards himself, without telling me. They are vulgar, expensive things from Smirkson's, and he was angry at having bought a bad bargain. In the circumstances, I said nothing about my 'Darwitts'' cards, but put them away in the sideboard, under the knife box. They will come in next year.

DECEMBER 21. Sat together at the dining table, selecting and addressing our cards – always one of the most pleasurable tasks of the year; though marred on this occasion by Lupin, who is very low-spirited and disagreeable these days. When Charlie said something to the effect of his 'having got off a very bad bargain,' in respect of Daisy Mutlar, Lupin practically jumped down his throat, and snapped that Daisy was 'worth the whole bunch of his father's friends put together, that inflated sloping-head of a Perkupp included.' When we were alone, Charlie blamed his offensive disrespect for Mr Perkupp on my example, saying: 'It is you he gets it from, Carrie.' I said: 'Whatever our son may have "got", Charlie, he has got not from me, nor from you, *but from Daisy Mutlar.*'

As we resumed addressing our cards, Charlie gave me the opportunity to dispose of a matter that has been causing me some worry. He said: 'Shall we send one to the Griffins next door?'

I said: 'No, dear.'

He said: 'Why not? You and Mrs Griffin have called on one another.'

I said: 'I know, but I think instead of a card she would expect a calendar with our name and address printed on it.'

Charlie said: 'In gold leaf, I shouldn't wonder! Then she will be disappointed. We are not that kind of people.'

It is a weight off my mind.

DECEMBER 22. I was taking down my hair before going to bed, when there was a knock, and Charlie entered. He said: 'I thought I had best come up and give you the news at once, Carrie. Lupin has just told me that *the engagement is on again.*'

I said: 'I know it is.'

He said: '*How* do you know? Did he tell you?'

I said: 'There is such a phenomenon as a mother's instinct. Besides, why, should you suppose, has he started using bay rum again?'

*Another bangle for Christmas. A pleasant little holiday
at Mother's − we meet a scullery-maid in training,
who will go far. Our super-abundance of 'Xmas cards.
My musical soirée ends as a fiasco. I break a New
Year resolution.*

13

DECEMBER 24. Since we always go to Mother's, near Reading, for Christmas, and Lupin will be staying at the Mutlars', I have done nothing towards decorating the house, beyond bringing down the festive table-place garlands – holly-wreaths cut out of card – which we fetched home with us, the year we went to the Subscription Christmas Dinner of the Peckham Mock Parliament. They still look very pretty, if a little dog-eared by now.

Charlie exasperated me at this eleventh hour by asking what I would like for 'Xmas – he had requested Zimmerman Bros to put by the amethyst beads that I liked, but despite his having left a deposit, there had been a misunderstanding, and they had sold them. I said: 'What I should really like, in that event, is one of the smaller "Wenham Lake" ice safes, from Merryweather's.' From his reply, I do not think I shall get it.

Much huffing and puffing over an 'insulting' Christmas card he had received. He would not show it to me, but locked it away in his deed box. It is one of the cheapjack comic cards they are selling at Batchford's, the tobacconist's, where I purchased Charlie's 'Xmas cigars – a crude representation of a pair of geese alongside a set of kitchen scales; the accompanying message being: ' "NO TAKERS" FOR WHICH OF US IS THE "PRIZE" ONE.' Vulgar, yes; but I would not say insulting, except in the mind of one lacking in any sense of fun. Besides, it is quite plain, to anyone not in a rage, that it is addressed to the 'L' and not the 'C,' of the 'Pooters Esq' in this house; from which it may be concluded that Frank

Mutlar is the culprit, and Lupin his true victim. There is nothing I can say to Charlie, without revealing that his deed box will unlock with a hairpin; I can only hope that the truth will dawn upon him, sooner or later.

CHRISTMAS DAY. Charlie gave me a bangle. A charming little thing, but I shall soon have enough bangles to start a hoop-la stall. I gave him a 'United Services' patent trousers stretcher – his knees do bag so. Lupin having declared: 'Definition of a Christmas gift: that which nobody wants, proffered by one who has no inclination to give it; and then reciprocated – all this in order to *avoid* giving what no man in his senses would have dreamt of taking – offence!' we neither of us dared buy him anything. Yet, and not withstanding his further strictures upon 'the great Christmas present racket,' Lupin came down to breakfast with a box of expensive bon-bons for me, and hair brushes for his father. I whispered in Charlie's ear, who saved the day for us by presenting Lupin with the box of cigars which I always get for him, to take down to Reading.

Caught the 10.20 train from Paddington. Mother well enough, considering, apart from a peffing cough, for which she is taking American Cherry Pectoral. Most of the usual company at mid-day dinner: dear old Revd Panzy Smith, of St Chad's, who married us; my cousins Jessie, Oriel and Edward, from Maidenhead and district; Mother's neighbours, who are Mr and Mrs Jepp; and a young Mr Moss, who has taken the place at Christmas table of old Miss Maude, now sadly demised. Mother hopes Mr Moss may set his cap at Jessie: I fear not – that shelf is too high. Charlie took umbrage because Mr Moss, taking it upon himself to kiss the ladies under a sprig of mistletoe, thought to include me. I said: 'Had he left me out, we should have both taken umbrage.'

In the evening, we had Mother to ourselves, when we got out the cards and played game after game of 'Napoleon,' for which she has formed a passion.

DECEMBER 26. Mr Jepp kindly carried Mother and me in his dog-cart to the Female Orphan Working School, to present the rag dolls which she makes during the year, for the poor girls. Mother's fingers being not as nimble as they were, she was able this year to manage only five dolls. If the Warden, Mr Strains, was disappointed, he disguised it very well. Mr Strains sent for one of the senior girls, Nelly, to accept the dolls; she curtseyed very nicely and made a little speech of thanks. She is a bright and personable girl: Mr Strains told us that she is earmarked for a scullery-maid at one of the big houses. It will not be many months before Nelly is serving above stairs, if I am any judge of character.

Back to Town on the 6.40. The carriage reeked of peppermint.

DECEMBER 27. This year, for the first time ever, we have received more 'Xmas cards than we sent out. The mantelpiece is a veritable forest of them. Not counting those addressed exclusively to Lupin (including Charlie's 'insulting' one, which, after much dark and solitary brooding, he now realizes was never meant for him!), we have 26. Had Mr Gowing reciprocated our card – I know he will swear that he did, and that it 'must have been lost in the post' – there should have been 27. Those to whom we have omitted to send cards are: Mrs Shrike, of Bow; Mr and Mrs Treane (last year we sent to them, but they failed to send to us – I wish they would only make up their minds); and Mr Gomersall, the under-manager of Throstle & Epps' Linen Bank, Oldham (we debated the pros and cons of striking Mr Gomersall off our list long and earnestly; evidently we were wrong in our conclusion that such social obligations as we may have had towards him – we have never met – ceased upon Lupin taking his leave of the Bank).

There is nothing to be done about Mrs Shrike, since I lack her address. I despatched New Year cards to the others.

DECEMBER 28. Daisy and Frank Mutlar, Mr Cummings and Mr Gowing to supper. As habitually when young Mr Mutlar is our guest, the evening degenerated rapidly into tomfoolery, with much throwing of bread pellets and parsley, turning on and off of gas, and the remainder. To restore order, I suggested an impromptu musical soirée around our cottage piano – never mind that this let the company in for another four ballads from Daisy (she had already treated us to four before supper). I sang 'The Garden of Sleep,' of which Charlie says he never tires; whilst Lupin and Frank Mutlar gave us 'the latest thing' – 'So I strolled about the Park once more', which they took verse and verse about; and Mr Gowing rendered a music-hall ditty, 'Give me a 'ot potato, do!' which, although vulgar, was not offensively so. Mr Cummings contributed a duet which he said he often sings at home with his wife; since Mrs Cummings did not honour us with her presence, he was obliged to take both parts, and sounded ridiculous. He did not volunteer any explanation as to why Mrs Cummings chose not to be with us to take the soprano role herself.

There was then much 'egging on' of Charlie to give us something, not to be 'the odd man out,' or 'such an old fogey,' as Lupin disrespectfully put it. To my utter astonishment, he capitulated – the first time I have ever known such a thing. He elected to sing something from *The Pirates of Penzance*, which we attended at the Opéra Comique, to celebrate our pewter wedding. I did not have the music, but said I would follow as best I could. What I did not know was how little Charlie knew the words. The effect was calamitous. He had got no farther than:

I am the very model of a modern Major-General,
I-ve rumpty-tumpty vegetable, animal and mineral;
I know the something something and the tiddley-idle
  rumpty-al
From Waterloo to Waterloo in order mathematical –

– when the cat-calling and throwing down of halfpence

132

began. Mr Gowing pelted Charlie with cough lozenges from a paper bag. Even Mr Cummings, who is usually above that sort of thing, tossed a 'bouquet' of pot-pourri, with the cry: 'Bravo! The George Grossmith of Holloway!'

I'll warrant that a veil is drawn over this portion of the evening in dear old Charlie's diary.

DECEMBER 30. Over supper, Lupin fulminated against Mr Mutlar, Senr, calling him 'an old fool' and many other things besides – he is 'stingy,' 'practices farthing economy' and so on and so on. Charlie remonstrated, but mildly. When Lupin had gone out of the room, I said: 'You let him off lightly.' Charlie said: 'Canute could not turn back the tide, Carrie. It is the way young folk talk now-a-days.' I said: 'Then I wonder what Frank Mutlar says about *you*, dear.' He grew very thoughtful.

DECEMBER 31. These are my New Year resolutions:

1. To be less sharp with my dear husband. He knows I hardly ever mean it, and that I will sometimes make a remark for the sake of seeming clever, just as he will make one in the hope of seeming witty; but I must not let my tongue run away with me.

The effect was calamitous

133

2. To make an effort to discover those qualities in Daisy Mutlar, that recommend her to Lupin; failing which, to keep my opinions to myself. I have caught myself being disagreeable about her to Lupin just lately.

3. To discourage the belief in some quarters that 'The Laurels' is 'open house' – Mr Gowing, in particular, to be disabused of this notion; and Mr Cummings to be enquired of, each and every time he sits down at my table, whether Mrs Cummings is unwell.

4. To acquire a 'Wenham Lake' ice safe, even if I have to serve rancid mutton all summer long.

Charlie decanted a bottle of 'Lockanbar' with which to see the Old Year out. There was some brandy in the other decanter – provided by Lupin, with the declaration that 'he is sick of the gargle-mixture provided in this house.' As the witching hour approached, Charlie poured two measures of what he thought to be whisky – I knew very well it was brandy: I could tell by the smell. An argument ensued, in the course of which I regret to say I made some cruel and spiteful comments as to my husband's dulled palate. I then saw, to my distress, that it was a quarter of an hour into the New Year. My first resolution shattered already.

Charlie's promotion below my expectations – but his increment far above them. Shopping at Merryweather's and elsewhere. Lupin's good fortune. Sarah attempts to give notice. A disappointment as regards Mr Darwitts. The absence of Mr Gowing.

14

JANUARY 1. Important and thrilling news. Mr Buckling, the chief book-keeper at Perkupp & Co., is to retire, and Charlie has been informed, by Mr Perkupp, in person, in so many words, that he is to be promoted, with a substantial increase in salary.

It is not before time. Year after year, Charlie has been passed over for advancement. Unlike the rest of the pack, he has steadfastly refused to 'blow his own trumpet,' with the result that he has been overlooked, whilst the Mr Bucklings of this world have got on in leaps and bounds. Yet a steady light cannot be hidden for ever under a bushel. At last, Charles Pooter's day has come!

He has promised that I shall have the velveteen costume which I saw at Peter Robinson's.

JANUARY 3. Two days now, and still no word as to what Charlie's new position is to be, or the extent of his increment. Mr Perkupp is keeping him on tenterhooks deliberately. I have told him to march into Mr Perkupp's room and demand to know where he stands, but he will not, being Charlie. In his place, I should shake Mr Perkupp until his teeth rattled.

JANUARY 4. And so it comes to this: he is not to succeed Mr Buckling – that plum goes to Mr Davidge, the chief clerk. Mr Spotch steps into Mr Davidge's shoes, and Charlie into Mr Spotch's.

I said: 'So after all this, you have been made no more than a senior clerk?'

He said: 'It would appear so.'

I said: 'I thought you had been that all along.'

He said: 'It would appear not.'

He still does not know what his new salary is to be. Poor, dear Charlie! I had not the heart to ask him why he had not the wit to enquire, whilst he had Mr Perkupp's ear.

Altogether a disturbing day. I have learned from Charlie's diary that Mr Mutlar has written to him, forbidding Lupin his house. He had said not a word about it to me. I cannot abide secrecy between man and wife; moreover, I was anxious to know how this banishment left Lupin with Daisy; and so I put it to Charlie point-blank: 'Why, do you suppose, is Lupin no longer at the Mutlars' each evening?' Upon this, he showed me the letter, wherein Mr Mutlar takes exception to Lupin's irrepressible demeanour. It is a pity, if he wishes to sit in judgement upon the exuberant manners of the young, that he did not put his own house in order first. Charlie had it out with Lupin: the position with Daisy is that she will wait for him ten years, if necessary – or so he wishes to believe.

JANUARY 5. I can scarcely believe it. Charlie's salary is to be increased by *one hundred pounds a year*! He was expecting £20 at most – for myself, I thought he would be fobbed off with £15. I said: 'It is an inducement, to prevent you throwing down your pen and taking a position elsewhere, who would recognise your abilities and appoint you at once to what you should have been this many a year – chief clerk.' Charlie said: 'No, dear, it is the reward for twenty-one years' tireless and faithful service to a good master.' He makes himself sound like a drayhorse.

We celebrated with champagne. Lupin somewhat took the gilt off our gingerbread by announcing that he too had some good news: he has made £200 on £5-worth of stocks and shares – I forget in what – given to him by his employer, Mr Job Cleanands.

One hundred pounds! Two hundred pounds! My head swims – and not only from the champagne.

JANUARY 7. Shopping. First to Merryweather's, where I ordered a new chimney-glass for the drawing room; and obtained an illustrated price-list of the 'Wenham Lake' prize medal ice safes. Unlike the older model, which I saw going into 'The Larches,' they are now fitted with the new American butter dish with revolving lid. Ice may be delivered at a cost of less than a penny per pound.

Thence to Peter Robinson's, where I tried on the velveteen costume; but plum does not suit me in such quantity, and they did not have it in any other colour – perhaps I shall ask Annie Fullers (now Mrs James, of Sutton) to copy it in bottle green. But I did buy a 'Mandleburg' waterproof, and a pair of kid opera gloves. I also bought a pair of Armstrong's 'Jubilee' braces for Charlie, and a collapsible hat for Lupin. Looked at some of the furniture in Heal's, where I took morning coffee and a macaroon.

JANUARY 9. Charlie has set his face against the 'Wenham Lake' and every other brand of ice safe.

I said: 'Mr Griffin, next door, has bought one, and Mrs Griffin swears by it.'

Charlie said: 'Then Mr Griffin must have more money than sense.'

I said: 'The only money Mr Griffin has, is what he has earned with hand and brain.' (Sarah, my maid, has learned that he is a 'self-made man' – a fruit and vegetable wholesaler with his own small warehouse.)

Charlie said: 'Pardon me for contradicting you, Carrie, but the only money any man has, is what he has saved.'

I could see that he was pleased with this observation; and so I asked quickly if I might have a new dress, to make up for the costume in Peter Robinson's which I never bought, and he cheerfully agreed that I might.

He has only just realised that he is going bald

JANUARY 20. Lupin intends to hire a pony-trap, he is doing so well for himself – he manages (I do not quite understand how, but it is to do with buying and selling stocks or shares) to earn far and away above what he is paid in simple salary.

I said anxiously: 'I hope you are not "riding for a fall"!'

Lupin said: 'Don't worry, ma. I only go on Job Cleanands' tips, and he knows his onions.'

I said: 'I was thinking of the pony-trap. Don't tell your father about it.'

He said; 'Have a heart – it's not the kind of thing a fellow can keep dark!'

I said: 'Then don't tell him today. He has only just realised that he is going bald.'

JANUARY 22. Sarah (my maid) gave notice, for the reason that 'the Master 'ad been picking on her; it 'ad been pick, pick, pick, all breakfuss-time long.' I did hear Charlie complaining to her about his egg, and other matters that are none of his business. I have half a mind to let her go, and hire a proper lady's maid at twice her money, through Crookston & Parfitt's agency in The Strand; but Sarah has been with us for so long, and so much knows our little ways, that for all her failings I could not bear to part with her. I gave her a florin and packed her off to her sister's at The Borough for the night, telling her not to be so silly. A plate of brawn for supper, was not well received by Charlie. He will like brawn for breakfast even less.

JANUARY 24. To Darwitts', wholesale stationers &c &c, in the Clerkenwell Road, to enquire the cost of binding up my completed set of *Lady Cartmell* in blue cloth with deckled edges. Whilst I waited at the trade counter, Mr Darwitts came out, every bit as tall and straight-backed as I remember him. He returned my bow, but looked mystified.

I said: 'I am sure you haven't forgotten the Lord Mayor's Ball already, Mr Darwitts!'

He said: 'Forgive me, dear lady – I was lost in a brown study. It's Mrs Twentyman, is it not?'

I said: 'Mrs Pooter.'

He said: 'Of course. How are you, Mrs Pooter?'

Unaccountably, I was seized by what Lupin would call 'a fit of the blues' on the 'bus home; but cheered up when I saw that the new chimney-glass for our drawing room has arrived. I expended some time and care on arranging fans around it; and very nice it looks.

JANUARY 25. Mr Cummings called for the first time in weeks, having been ill, so he informs us. He grumbled that no-one had noticed his absence. I said: 'I noticed, for one, Mr Cummings.'

Mr Gowing also came round. Wonders will never cease: he has invited us, and the Cummings', to supper tomorrow. In all the time we have known him – and I go back to the days when he had rooms around the corner from us in Peckham (he now has rooms around the corner from us in Holloway, having 'upped sticks' the moment he learned that we were removing) – we have never once sat down at his table. I wonder who is going to lay it for him.

JANUARY 26. To Mr Gowing's, where we met Mr and Mrs Cummings – but not, however, Mr Gowing. He was out, having gone to Croydon for the weekend. Charlie and Mr Cummings were furious. For my part, I was rather amused; an evening without Mr Gowing's company is a deprivation I can tolerate. But I *should* have liked to have seen the state of his rooms.

A sharp difference of opinion regarding the growth of hair. At my wits' end over the laundering – think of an ingenious solution, but not one that my husband would entertain. My first and last drive in Lupin's pony-cart. The game of 'Curtailments and Retailings'. We meet Lupin's rival. Mutilation of my Lady Cartmell, by Darwitts'.

15

FEBRUARY 6. Charlie's birthday, which was uneventful. He never did like a fuss being made of it; but now that his hair is growing thinner by the day, he refuses to observe it at all. I bowed to his wishes, and discouraged Lupin from sending him a card, which would most surely have been of the 'comical' variety; but I did feel that the occasion should be marked in some small way, and so as a token I gave him a bottle of 'Koko' hair tonic. This led, unexpectedly, to an argument.

Studying the label, Charlie said suddenly: 'Hulloh! This is no good! You have bought me a *ladies*' preparation!'

There is certainly a picture of a girl on the bottle, but I could not see what difference it made. I said: 'Hair is hair, Charlie. "Koko" is just as efficacious for men as for women.'

Charlie said: 'Men's hair is utterly different from women's hair, Carrie, believe me – otherwise all the ladies would have beards. We don't know what might happen to my hair if I try this stuff!'

I said: 'We know what will happen to it if you don't. You are losing enough each day to stuff a cushion!' I wish I had not spoken so on his birthday, but he can be so exasperating.

FEBRUARY 9. The laundress having missed two of her days, she now has all of Charlie's collars except the one he is wearing. She should have brought back three collars today, but has brought none. 'It ain't that they are lost' – I am to mark! – 'She is sure she can put her 'ands on them, but not just at present.' What this means is that one of her clientele is walking about London wearing my husband's collars.

I am at my wits' end, having by now gone through every laundress in Holloway. I have tried giving socks and collars to Mrs Birrell, but the collars come back with fingermarks all over them, and the socks stiff as boards, from the soap she has failed to rinse out. Sarah (my maid) will not do the work. She says she would consider it, if we had one of the self-acting washing machines from Merryweather's, which save £10 a year in laundering bills.

I considered putting it to Charlie, that the £10 we should save from possessing a self-acting washing machine, could be invested in a 'Wenham Lake' ice safe; whilst with the money we should save from possessing the ice safe, by not having to throw foodstuffs away, we could pay for the self-acting washing machine. But he would only pooh-pooh the idea, and say that I know nothing about commerce.

I made Charlie buy six new collars, and marked them with Raddles' ink whilst he held them in front of the fire to dry them. Mr Gowing came in and gave us a cock-and-bull tale to account for his absence from his own supper table a fortnight ago – something about having to go to Croydon, and a letter informing us of the fact going astray. I whispered to Charlie, that a likelier explanation was that he had put our chops on to cook, and dropped them in the fire. We both roared at this, to Mr Gowing's mystification; and then I saw that Charlie had scorched every one of his six new collars.

FEBRUARY 10. Lupin took us for a drive in his pony-cart. I would as soon go up in a hot-air balloon as repeat the experience. He has taken no instructions at all in driving, beyond a turn around Highgate Ponds with Frank Mutlar. He did not inform me of this fact until we were careering towards Highgate Archway like a fire

'Make way for Boadicea!'

engine, passing every cab and cart we came across. When I expressed my apprehension, he called out airily: 'O, pooh – any fool can drive, ma!' I said: 'I know *one* who can't!' I then urged him to turn back and take us home. Grabbing the reins to underline this request, I tugged more sharply than I intended, and we mounted the pavement for a short distance. To passers-by, it must have looked as if I were driving, for a street-arab cried: 'Make way for Boadicea!' Meantime, on the back-seat, Charlie was being pelted with orange peel by a gang of roughs following us in a donkey-cart.

We must have looked a pretty sight as we alighted, back at 'The Laurels' – I with my hat askew, like a tipsy slattern reeling home from a gin-palace, Charlie spattered with mud, as if having been picked up out of the gutter. Although trembling from head to foot, I refused the arms of my husband and son – I knew what it would have looked like to Mrs Griffin, whose bedroom curtain I observed twitching. I hope she did not see me stumble on a loose flag as Lupin held open the gate.

FEBRUARY 11. From the pages of *Pot-Pourri: A Weekly Miscellany For Ladies*, which I am taking in now that *Lady Cartmell* has run her course, I learned a game, new to me, called 'Curtailments and Retailings.' I attempted to initiate Charlie into it. A word, which is concealed in a clever clue, must first be revealed, and then curtailed by its last letter, to make another word, to which a clue is likewise provided. An example given by 'The Sphinx' (*Pot-Pourri*'s contributor) is: 'Curtail the animals of a given species, and find one who is half animal, half man.' The answers are *Fauna* and *Faun*. I myself thought up quite a good one: 'Curtail the table, and it becomes a wild pig.' The answers are *Board* and *Boar*.

Charlie either could not, or would not, understand the game. He failed to solve any of the examples I set for him, and the nearest he got to a proper example of his own was: 'Curtail what one climbs, and they become what twinkle.' Answers: *Stairs* and *Stars*. I explained, for the nth time, that the curtailed letter *must* be taken from the end of the word; and was teaching him the rules once more, when Mr Gowing turned up, with a game he has found known as 'Pin The Tail On The Donkey'. We spent the rest of the evening blindfolding one another to the point of tedium. Charlie cried: 'This is more our style, Carrie!' and laughed himself silly. Now there are pin-pricks all over a good square yard of expensive flock wall-paper.

Lupin has given up his pony and trap; or the pony and trap has given him up – I mind not which.

FEBRUARY 12. Looking out of the first landing window after Lupin had gone off this morning, saw him standing at the corner, where presently he hailed a cab to take him down to the office. Have not troubled to mention this to Charlie – although for all I know, having invested some money on our son's advice, he may soon enough be riding to business in cabs himself.

Frank Mutlar called this evening, bringing with him Mr Murray Posh, of 'Posh's three-shilling hat' fame, a tall, plump young man of prosperous appearance. He wore a diamond pin, which was certainly not 'paste,' as Charlie, affecting a knowledge of precious stones, tried to make out when he had gone. Mr Posh talked a great deal about hats; but a great deal more about Daisy Mutlar, with whom he seems very intimate. Frank Mutlar made a curious, although joshing, remark to Lupin: 'If you don't look out, "Loopy," Posh will cut you out!' When, later, his father referred to this flippant observation, Lupin said with a sneer: 'A man who would be jealous of an elephant like Murray Posh could only have a contempt for himself.' I know my son, and I know a little of the ways of the world. *He is jealous of Murray Posh – who will cut him out with Daisy Mutlar.*

FEBRUARY 13. My bound-up volume of *Lady Cartmell's Vade Mecum For the Bijou Household* was delivered this morning. It *looks* handsome enough, with the title nicely blocked in gold, and the deckling not skimped; but upon opening it and browsing through it, I found that in trimming the pages, the binder has cut too deeply into the margin – the consequence being that in those numbers where the outer margin was unusually narrow, all the word-endings at the edge of the page have been shaved off. This is particularly evident in the chapter on 'The Drug Cabinet & Home Doctor,' which is so guillotined as to be incomprehensible. I showed the botched volume to Charlie, thinking that he would sit down at once and compose one of his satirical letters to Darwitts'. Instead, he only chuckled and said: 'Just like your game of "Curtailments"!'

I shall never deal with that firm again.

My admirer sends me a Valentine. The Misses Tipper call again, bringing with them an unhappy dog. We have a run of bad luck; but then our fortunes change. Lupin disengaged in two senses of the word.

16

FEBRUARY 14. It is a marvel now-a-days for Charlie to remember St Valentine's Day. Last evening I got out the plush-covered album in which I keep my most precious cards and paper mementoes, and was quietly leafing through it, when Charlie rose abruptly and said; 'Do you know, Carrie, I have a mind to take a turn up the street and back.'

I said: 'But it's raining.'

He said: 'It is only a drizzle, and I have a slight head-ache.'

I said: 'If you pass the fancy-stationers', you might bring me back some bun-cases.'

He said: 'I shan't be going near the fancy-stationers'.'

Bun-cases came there none – but a beautiful Valentine card, of quilted sateen, lace-edged, and with a verse to make one blush, arrived by this morning's first post. Charlie steadfastly denied having sent it, saying with a twinkle: 'I can think of not only one, but several, admirers who might have done, however.'

I said: 'But they didn't.'

Charlie said: 'A-ha – you will never be sure,' and turned to his newspaper. What a dear man he is: it goes without saying, that if he *hadn't* sent the card, I should never hear the last of it.

Lupin also received a card, but threw it straight into the fire – it is to be assumed that it was of the 'insulting' kind.

FEBRUARY 18. Whilst engaged in scraping strands of

hair over his bald patch, Charlie dropped a hand-glass and broke it; added to which, his enlarged photograph in the drawing room, which I have told him time without number needs a stronger cord, fell down at last, cracking the glass. I warned him that misfortune was about to befall us. He pooh-poohed the presentiment. I reminded him of what happened when Annie Fullers (now Mrs James, of Sutton) brought up her 'Oracle of Delphi' fortune teller, and it predicted 'an accident.' Charlie was eloquent in his ridicule; laughing scornfully, he made to walk out of the room – and sprawled headlong over Annie's parasol.

The hand-glass was bought for me by Lupin, and so I knew that he must be tied up in our misfortune in one way or another. This evening he came home in a state of agitation and revealed that the stocks and shares he had advised his father to buy, to the tune of £20, had crashed, and he is fortunate to have recovered £2. One reads of such calamities in shilling novels: I never thought it could happen to us.

FEBRUARY 19. The Misses Tipper called, bringing with them a Collie dog of very morose appearance, named Claude. Cinders, our little cat, would have gone for him, but he was so wretched and docile that she was put to shame, and suffered herself to be banished below stairs without demur. He is not the Misses Tippers' dog: he belongs to a friend of theirs, a Mrs Batch, on whose behalf (Mrs Batch cannot get about) they were taking him to see their brother, the veterinary practitioner, as he is listless and off his food. He did not look at all happy, and refused a crust of malt loaf.

The Misses Tipper asked if they might see over the house. This was a most unexpected request, since they have already seen over it from top to bottom. My surprise must have conveyed itself to the sisters, for Miss Tipper Jnr added: '. . . now that you have got everything as you would wish it.' Their inspection was even more thorough than before; and Miss Tipper Senr evinced great interest in how we had got the big wardrobe up the stairs without sawing it in half. Claude lumbered dolefully after us from room to room. At first, I was afraid that he was going to knock over an ornament or knick-knack, and add to our breakages; in the end, I almost wished that he would: the experience might have raised his spirits.

Upon taking their leave, the Misses Tipper asked if they might bring Oswald (the brother) over one afternoon, as he has his practice very close by, in Carthby Terrace. I said that of course I should be delighted.

The house more than ever resembled a gentleman's club this evening – if the gentleman's club exists that would admit Mr Gowing. First of all, Charlie and Lupin, smoking cigars, went importantly into the parlour and closed the door. I could not follow much of their earnest talk, but it was to the effect that Mr Gowing and Mr Cummings were as much involved as Charlie in the stocks and shares 'crash' – as to which, it appears, the non-appearance of Mr Job Cleanands to 'face the music' is causing some dismay. Then, just as Lupin was about to hurry out of the house, Mr Gowing arrived. The three men closeted themselves in the parlour, and again the door closed. Presently I was surprised to hear laughter.

Claude

Again I understood very little of what was being said; except that neither Mr Gowing nor Lupin himself, after all, are victims of the 'crash' – Mr Gowing because 'he smelled turbot' and 'unloaded' his stocks and shares upon poor Mr Cummings; and Lupin because he never bought any for himself in the first place. This latter revelation seemed to annoy Charlie; I thought he would be pleased for the boy.

Finally, Mr Cummings came, looking upset. For all that the parlour door had hitherto not opened, it was by Charlie alone that Mr Cummings was received when he knocked upon it – Lupin and Mr Gowing having beaten a retreat by a most unconventional means.

Later, Charlie, very bad-tempered and wishing to pick a quarrel, said: 'Why are there dog hairs all over the house?'

I said: 'For the same reason as there are footprints on my freshly donkey-stoned parlour window sill – we have had visitors.'

FEBRUARY 20. It is my contention that blessings, like misfortunes, come in threes; and that if only one will believe this, the good immediately follows upon the bad. We have had our three misfortunes – Charlie's £20 all but wiped out; a dish of potato fritters last evening that was an utter failure (hot raisin-wine sauce sickly, and blistered our lips); and this morning I caught a fish-fork in my coral beads, and scattered them. I said to Charlie: 'Now we have had the three bad things, fortune will turn over a new leaf and send us three good things.'

Charlie said: 'Nonsense, dear.' He thereupon opened his newspaper and read: 'Great Failure of Stock and Share Dealers! Mr Job Cleanands Absconded!'

I said: 'That is the first blessing.'

Charlie said: 'I fail to see what is good about the disappearance of Lupin's employer.'

I said: 'It is good for Lupin. Mr Cleanands was never a good influence.'

Then the subject of this exchange came downstairs.

The news did not surprise him at all; but he had some news of his own with which he thought to surprise his parents – and perhaps did surprise one of them.

Lupin said carelessly; 'O, by-the-by. Daisy Mutlar is to be married next month, to Murray Posh, the "three-shilling-hats" chap.'

I mouthed to Charlie, as we ate our breakfast in silence: 'That is the second.'

As he was leaving for the office, Charlie said: 'Very well, Carrie; you see before you a convert. What is the third?'

I said: 'We shall be having a nice bottle of "Jackson Frères" champagne with our supper – provided you remember to buy it.'

Vexed by the Great Northern Railway. An accident to our plaster of Paris stag's head. The Mutlar – Posh wedding. Lupin is taken into Mr Perkupp's office, whereat I day-dream of Pooter & Father on a brass plate.

17

MARCH 2. This mid-morning a railway train broke down at the bottom of our garden, and was there for a good half-hour, belching steam at us until the house resembled a vapour bath. Charlie questioned me keenly as to the time of the incident. Thinking he meant to write one of his satirical letters to the directors of the company, I went to the trouble of seeking out Sarah (my maid) to corroborate my impression that it was at about eleven o'clock. Looking importantly at his watch, Charlie said: 'In that case, it will almost certainly have been the 9.25 from Royston.' He fills his head with such useless details, and reads *Bradshaw* for hours, even though we never go anywhere. Since he appeared to think this was the end of the matter, I said sharply: 'I do not care if it was the night mail from Glasgow. If this is how it is to be, I would sooner live in a tent on Farringdon Station.'

MARCH 8. I hope that Lupin is not taking the Daisy Mutlar business too much to heart. We see little of him: he sleeps all morning, goes out in the afternoon to canvass his City friends for any situation that might have come to their ears; and spends his evenings at music-halls. Last night he came in very late, singing that he was 'quite all right, and fit as a tick, on Esmerelda's elder brother's elderberry wine.' He continued to sing long after he must have gone to bed. I do not like Lupin singing in bed: it is not healthy.

MARCH 9. One of the antlers of our plaster of Paris

stag's head was broken off when I came down this morning. Sarah (my maid) told me that she had found it on the floor, together with Lupin's stick. We surmised that he must have hung his stick up on the stag's head when he came in last night, the umbrella stand being full (we have a surfeit of sticks and umbrellas at present, belonging mainly to Mr Cummings and Mr Gowing. I wonder they do not leave their boots to be soled). Happily, Charlie did not notice, and I got to work with the Prout's Elastic Glue the minute he had left the house.

MARCH 11. I am very fearful that Charlie is about to ask

I got to work with the Prout's Elastic Glue

Mr Perkupp to take Lupin into his office, as a favour. I must resign myself to it: the fact of having had the misfortune to have been in the employ of 'Job "Clean-'em-out" Cleanands' (as the halfpenny papers now dub the scallawag) is a millstone around Lupin's neck in his search for a position. Yet I feel as the wives of colliers must do, when their sons are obliged to follow their fathers into the pit-cage. The prospects are grim indeed. Either Lupin will be kept down, on a junior clerk's pay, just as Charlie was for so long, and will grow bitter; or else his innate abilities will drive him to the top, when he will be senior to his own father; and it will be Charlie who grows bitter. There are times when I wish we had encouraged Lupin's earliest ambition, and allowed him to go on the stage.

MARCH 14. Entering the breakfast parlour with slow tread, Charlie remained in pensive thought for a while, and then said: 'You know, Carrie, it is a remarkable thing. We have had our plaster of Paris stag's head for a good six months or more, yet I have only just noticed that one of its antlers is the wrong way round – I who pride myself on my powers of observation!'

I thought to chastise him for not examining his purchases more closely before parting with good money; but something held me back. Instead I said: 'No-one else has noticed it, dear, so you are not alone.'

MARCH 19. Daisy Mutlar's wedding day tomorrow. Lupin, whilst outwardly cheerful – always with a song on his lips – has the demeanour of a condemned man. Tonight he stayed in and played euchre with his father. As the evening wore on, they fell to showing one another simple conjuring tricks. I almost felt, as I went to bed, that there should have been a warder sitting outside the door. But, for Lupin's sake, I must steel myself, and pray that there is no 'last-minute reprieve.'

MARCH 20. The marriage today of Miss Daisy Mutlar

and Mr Murray Posh, at St George's Church, is the subject of a brief paragraph in the Court & Social column of the *City Press* – the name of *Posh*, I fancy, rather than that of *Mutlar*, having recommended itself as worthy of insertion. I hid the paper under a cushion before Lupin came down. This he did early; and after breakfasting on fresh air, wisely suffered himself to be carried off to Gravesend for the day, by a friend.

As the hour of Daisy's nuptials approached, I began to wish I had gone with him, for the temptation to go and stand outside the Church grew well nigh irresistible. It was not Daisy's wedding I wished to observe – why should I? – only Daisy's wedding *dress*, that I might satisfy my curiosity as to how such a big-boned girl – woman, rather – with such square, beefy shoulders, would 'carry off' the satin and lace of the demure young bride, without giving the bridegroom's family and friends cause to think of an operatic diva about to render an aria. I would have given half-a-crown for a glimpse of Daisy in that dress – and another for a rummage through her 'going-away' trousseau. (They are off to Wimereux.)

There being no reason to coop myself up indoors, on this or any other day, I did at last venture out to the *Bon Marché*, to price their muffs. St George's being on the way – I was careful to walk on the other side – I was amazed to see the church deserted, although it needed but five minutes to the time of the wedding. I went back home and retrieved the *City Press* from under the cushion; what, in my haste to read the paragraph as I heard Lupin coming down the stairs, I had thought to be St George's, Hankinson Square, N., was in fact St George's, Hanover Square, W. Later, being restless, I walked out again; and coming across the newspaper booth under the railway arches, I glanced through as many evening papers as I could, until the vendor asked me, with unnecessary gruffness, if I wanted to buy one; but mention of the wedding was there none. It cannot have been such a grand affair, after all.

MARCH 21. A letter from Mr Perkupp to Charlie, asking him to take Lupin down to the office with him. I confess that after Charlie had got Lupin out of bed, and persuaded him to dress in something quiet for a change, and Lupin, in a gust of rage, had jumped up and down on his Posh's 'three-shilling' hat, and then put on the collapsible hat that I bought him (he would never wear it before), a tear stung my cheek as I brushed the loose hairs off Charlie's shoulders and the troublesome scurf off Lupin's, and they set off together, arm-in-arm. All my misgivings vanished; and I felt a surge of pride at my menfolk sallying forth as one to their City office, as I always dreamed that they should. It is true that in my day-dream, the office was that of *Pooter & Son*, and that can never be realised now. But Lupin will do well for himself at Mr Perkupp's, I know he will; and why, in the

Lupin jumped up and down on his Posh's 'three-shilling' hat

fullness of time, should he not strike out for himself? And if he does, why not *Pooter & Father*? It would be an unusual brass plate to encounter on an office door in Fenchurch Street or Crooked Friars, to be sure, but how my heart would swell at the sight of it.

Mr Cummings and Mr Gowing came over this evening, and we celebrated Lupin's appointment in 'Jackson Frères' champagne, for which I am developing quite a taste.

'All Fools' Day' at the breakfast table. I perfect a recipe for 'mutton cakes', and submit it for publication. A worrying first encounter with Mr Oswald Tipper; followed by an intriguing second one. The East Acton Volunteer Ball, and its consequences.

18

APRIL 1. ALL FOOLS' DAY. Lupin played a clever trick upon his father at breakfast. Whilst Charlie was glancing down the obituaries column of his newspaper – he is assiduous about doing that, in case any friends of Mr Perkupp known to him should be mentioned – prior to attacking his second egg, Lupin surreptitiously removed the awaiting egg from beneath its cosy, and substituted in his father's egg-cup the shell of the egg which he had just devoured, unbroken side upwards, so that it looked like a whole egg. Charlie's face was a study, when he cracked that empty shell! 'April Fool, guv!' cried Lupin. We roared so loudly, and so long, that Sarah (my maid) came in to see what was the matter. Lupin said solemnly: 'O there you are, Sarah, you bad girl! What's a blue-bottle doing in the butter?' With a shriek, Sarah, cried: 'Oh, there never is, Mr Lupin!', and grabbed the lid off the butter dish. There was no bluebottle there, of course, Chorus: 'April Fool, Sarah!'

Then it was *my* turn to be 'caught out.' Sarah having left the room, Charlie said with wonderfully simulated crossness: 'I wish you had said something to Sarah about her failure to wind up the clock again, Carrie! See – it is nearly an hour slow!' Needless to say, when I turned towards the mantelpiece, and found the clock not wrong by a minute, it was to a cry of: 'April Fool!'

So passed as jolly a breakfast hour as I can remember. Still chortling, and trying to 'catch' one another – but we were all very wary by now! – Charlie and Lupin departed for the office, arm-in-arm, and smoking cigars.

Charlie and Lupin departed for the office

I hope there is to be no foolery at Mr Perkupp's expense – Charlie confides that Lupin is getting along very well, so far.

APRIL 8. Invented a new dish – 'mutton cakes.' The cold mutton being, as I knew, too 'marbley' for Charlie's queasy stomach, I made Sarah (my maid) mince it finely, whilst I prepared an onion, faggot of herbs &c &c. I then made up patties of minced mutton as one would make up fish cakes, except with less potato ingredients; and then bread-crumbed them and fried them, as if they were fish cakes; and served them with parsley. Charlie pronounced them delicious, and said that they were the next best thing to 'Lamb cutlets *à la Reform*,' which he has on those rare occasions when he goes to Gosling's Chop-house, near the office.

APRIL 12. The Misses Tipper came, and introduced their brother, Mr Oswald Tipper, a gentleman of sallow complexion, gaunt of countenance and as thin as a flue-brush. He would take nothing but a cup of hot water, with which he swallowed a powder. Yet he was animated enough in conversation.

Mr Tipper asked: 'In the most general terms, Mrs Pooter, what is the rateable value of the houses hereabouts?'

I said: 'I know nothing about such things, Mr Tipper. You would have to ask my husband,'

Mr Tipper said: 'It is too high, I'll be bound, Mrs Pooter. The Poor Rate has become a scandal. Do you realise how much we are paying for the maintenance of lunatics, when there is not an asylum for miles?'

This striking me as men's talk, and unsuitable for my drawing room, I adroitly changed the subject with a reference to Cinders, our cat, who was purring contentedly on top of my sewing table. Mr Tipper being a veterinary practitioner, I told him how Cinders will eat all the brown bread she can get, and enquired as to whether this was unusual in a cat.

Mr Tipper said: 'I have a rule, Mrs Pooter, never to intrude my professional opinions into private conversation. But if you will fetch the animal to see me, I shall most happily give you a free consultation, as a friend of my sisters'. My mornings for cats are Wednesdays and Fridays, between 9 and 11 o'clock.'

I could not make out from this whether a large appetite for brown bread is a symptom of a feline disorder, or whether Mr Tipper was offering in general terms to examine Cinders, should she ever look off-colour. He being so firm in his delineation between private and professional talk, I did not care to ask for further enlightenment. It was most kind of Mr Tipper to speak as he did; but it is very worrying.

By the same token I also felt inhibited from making any enquiries after Mrs Batch's dog, Claude.

APRIL 13. Being invited to a grand ball given by the East Acton Rifle Brigade next Tuesday, I got the dress I wore at the Lord Mayor's reception out of its tissue-paper, and repaired the loose stitches in the sleeves and hem. What a year my 'Duchess of Albany' ball-gown has had! It no longer seems such an extravagance, when I think of the use I have had out of it. My only regret is that it is too décolleté to turn into an afternoon dress after its 'society' days are over. East Acton being very far, I shall wear my ottoman mantle over it, and have sent this to be steam-cleaned.

APRIL 15. Charlie voted my 'mutton cakes' even better than last week's. Copied out my recipe in a fair hand, and posted it to *Pot Pourri: A Weekly Miscellany For Ladies*, which pays 2/6 for each cookery tip or household hint printed. Nothing ventured, nothing gained!

APRIL 16. To the East Acton Volunteer Ball, at which I did not expect to know a soul – it was, after all, a five-shilling cab ride from the purlieus of Holloway (the cabman thought it should be ten). To my surprise, almost the first person we saw as we walked about the Drill Hall, was Mr Padge, who came to our house once with his friend Mr Gowing, and once without him. I have no great opinion of Mr Padge; but if one goes out in society, it is inevitable that one's path will cross and re-cross those of an ever-widening circle of acquaintances many times; and so it is as well to be civil. We went with Mr Padge at once into the supper room, which was plea-santly empty; and were joined at the groaning board by one Mrs Lupkin. So familiar was this lady that I won-dered, at first, whether we had met before, at this or that function, when perhaps I had made a more lasting impression upon her than she upon me – but after some moments I realised that this was Mrs Lupkin's naturally friendly manner.

We had quite a talk about names. I said, as we were helped to champagne and pigeon pie (everything was most lavishly done – I was amazed that there were not more diners): 'You will be amused to hear, Mrs *Lupkin*, that my maiden name was *Lupin*, and that my grown-up son has *Lupin* for his first name.'

Mrs Lupkin said: 'It used to be quite the fashion, Mrs Pooter. I have a friend who was a Miss Jellmott before her marriage, and she called her first-born Jellmott as his given name. Jellmott Atkinson – to my mind, it has quite an American ring about it.'

I said: 'That is most interesting, Mrs Lupkin, but the point I was trying to convey was as to the similarity of our names – between *Lupkin* and *Lupin*.'

Mrs Lupkin said: 'No, no – there is a "k" in my name. It is spelled L-U-P-K-I-N.'

I said: 'Yes, I realise that such is the case; but if there *were* no "k" in your name, then it would be Lupin; whereas, with the *addition* of a "k", my maiden name and my son's name would be Lupkin.'

Mrs Lupkin said: 'No, I respectfully disagree, Mrs Pooter. You would not call a boy Lupkin, any more than you would call him Pooter. Those are surnames, pure and simple; whereas Lupin and Jellmott *sound* like first names, even though they were not originally.'

Mr Padge, who was pouring champagne liberally, said: 'That's right,' and I felt that the subject was exhausted. We went on to talk about Southend, where Mrs Lupkin lives (she is spending the night at Ealing, with her cousins), and which she recommends heartily as a resort. By the end of the evening we were 'hitting it off' so well that Mrs Lupkin invited Charlie and me to stay with her in Southend! She would not take 'no' for an answer, and we have arranged to go down on Saturday week.

Altogether, the ball was a resounding success, notwithstanding my considerate husband's failure to dance with me, being too busy plying the ladies with ices and glasses of champagne in the supper-room. Withal, the company was good, and I enjoyed myself thoroughly. The only trifling misfortune was when a man, mistaking Charlie for a waiter, tapped him on the shoulder and said: 'You – I should like a knife and fork!' Charlie only had to say: 'So should I!' Instead, he went and got them.

Going home was a different matter. It was raining buckets; cabs were few and far between; and none of them wanted to go as far as Holloway. The cabman who at last agreed to take us said he would go no farther than 'The Angel' at Islington, where we would have to get another cab. The journey was dreadful, with the rain beating down and much of it getting inside the cab, which I did not discover until I saw – and felt! – that small puddles were forming in the folds of my ottoman mantle. At 'The Angel,' I dashed into a pawnshop doorway whilst Charlie paid off the cabman; or rather, whilst he failed to do any such thing; for he had not a penny on him. No more had I. How a man can be so brainless as to drag his wife to the other side of London with no money in his pockets by which to get her home safely again, is completely beyond me. The cabman was a brute, and there was an altercation, over which I prefer to draw a veil; and then we set off to walk the two miles to Holloway in the driving rain. Would that I could blot that experience out of my mind, also; but I have too tangible a memento of it – to wit, an ottoman mantle, only just steam-cleaned, that is a sodden, mud-caked floorcloth; and my 'Duchess of Albany' ball-gown that is fit only for tearing up into plate-rags. When next we are invited to a social occasion, I am afraid that there will be some costly preliminary expenditure for my foolish husband!

Later: I scribble this note in the margin, having only just perused Charlie's own account of the East Acton Volunteer Ball in his diary. The reason that he came home penniless was that the supper, which we thought was free – or we should certainly not have pressed Mr Padge to join us – cost £3 os 6d! (I should have known, since it was Mr Gowing who gave us the tickets.) Charlie scraped together all the money he had, but even then was nine shillings short, and had to give the manager his card. This humiliation he kept utterly to himself. Why will not husbands confide in their wives? If Charlie had

Would that I could blot the experience out of my mind

only told me how he was placed, I should have gone up to
Mr Padge and said: 'Pardon me, Mr Padge, but I will
trouble you for the cost of your supper!' Mrs Lupkin, of
course, was our guest; as were, presumably, the
numerous ladies who flocked around my husband when
they heard that he was 'standing treat'!

After the indignities he was made to suffer by this misunderstanding, it does not surprise me that Charlie finds
no space in his diary to relate how he was mistaken for a
waiter.

APRIL 17. Punched some holes in an old hatbox with a
bodkin, and conveyed Cinders, our cat, to Mr Oswald
Tipper's consulting rooms in Carthby Terrace. I must
say that Mr Tipper has a way with animals. Cinders sat
perfectly still whilst he looked at her teeth – something

175

she would never allow me to do. Finally Mr Tipper pronounced: 'This is a healthy cat, Mrs Pooter. Brown bread contains nourishment, and will do her no harm in reasonable quantities, particularly if dipped in a little extract of beef.'

I thanked Mr Tipper, and rose to leave, at the same time making a civil enquiry as to the Misses Tippers' health. Mr Tipper said: 'There is a matter concerning my sisters, and you also, Mrs Pooter, that I would like to discuss with you; but I make it a rule never to intrude private conversation into a professional consultation. Will you give me leave to call upon you on Friday week, at 3 o'clock?'

Full of curiosity, I said that I should look forward to receiving Mr Tipper.

APRIL 18. Without reference to me – I should have no knowledge of the matter, had I not chanced upon an entry in his diary – Charlie has had in Mr Putley to mend the cistern. Mr Putley, as he well knows, is not a plumber, but a painter and decorator. No good will come of this.

Annie Fullers (now Mrs James, of Sutton) called unexpectedly, having some business in Town. She has given up her dressmaking enterprise, which was far too exhausting for her and has now taken up a line in paper insects, crabs, lobsters, frogs, snakes and the remainder, with which to decorate mantelpiece drapes, or hang on the curtains, or what you will. She buys them in sheets from a Japanese Warehouse that Mr James has been having dealings with, and after cutting-out, folding and painting them, sells them to bazaars and fancy stationers'. It is a thriving little business, and Annie already has three women working for her – the same three women who used to work the sewing-machines. She brought some examples of her handiwork up with her, and we arranged them on the drawing room mantelpiece. They look very pretty, and are quite cheap, to say that they are ahead of the fashion. Annie says that they will soon be 'all the rage.'

Mr James is well. Annie tells me that a sixth sense drew him back from the buffalo-meat dog biscuit venture at the eleventh hour; and that he is now considering a partnership in a product to be known – it has yet to be decided – either as 'Coc-ee' or 'Coffoa,' a blend of coffee and cocoa powder, from a secret formula, with anti-dyspeptic properties.

APRIL 19. Mr Griffin, of 'The Larches,' called on Charlie, and in plain language acquainted us with the fact that his cistern, which adjoins ours, has had a hole bored through it, to enable the water to drain into ours. He said he would get Mr Farmerson to repair it, and send us the bill. I said, after Mr Griffin had gone: 'It is a pity you did not get Mr Farmerson to our cistern.' Charlie said: 'You told me after the Lord Mayor's Ball, in no uncertain terms, that I was never to allow him into the house.' I said: 'I didn't say anything about not allowing him on the roof. Are you going to send for him, or do you mean to give the job to a glazier this time?'

APRIL 22. Charlie made a fuss because he discovered me manicuring my nails with one of the new 'emery sticks,' which Annie Fullers (now Mrs James, of Sutton) left behind on her last visit. If I varnished them, as Annie has been known to do on occasion, he would have something to make a fuss about.

APRIL 23. Letter from Mrs Lupkin, saying how much she looks forward to seeing us on Saturday, and promising that 'we shall charge you half what you will have to pay at the Royal!' Mrs Lupkin, as we now see from her notepaper, proves to be the proprietor of 'Lupkin's Family & Commercial Hotel'!

Charlie sat down at once and composed one of his satirical letters, declining her 'kind invitation' after all. What he does not know, and what there is little to be gained from telling him, is that I have already written to

177

Charlie sat down at once and composed
one of his satirical letters

Mrs Lupkin, asking her to spend August Bank Holiday
with us, she having confessed to me that this was the one
time of year when Southend became too crowded for
her. I can only hope that she is too busy with her guests,
or that she loses our address.

My recipe for 'mutton cakes' not yet in *Pot Pourri: A
Weekly Miscellany For Ladies*. Doubtless this week's
issue of the journal 'went to press' before my effort was
received. Such recipes as are published, are quite
unremarkable.

Mr Oswald Tipper unfolds an audacious plan. Charlie bumps into an old school friend, with tiresome consequences. Two o'clock dinner at Muswell Hill, where I am made to feel unwelcome (albeit unintentionally). Charlie's 'ice safe' nightmare.

19

APRIL 26. I have been burning to know what Mr Oswald Tipper wants of me. The day proposed for his visit dawned at last, and he arrived at three punctually. After sipping a cup of hot water, he asked if he might see the garden. Although it was a bitterly cold day, with a wind blowing cinder dust up from the railway tracks, I could hardly say him nay, and so we went out. I was chilled to the bone; but Mr Tipper, for all his thin frame and the fact that he had on only a light frock coat, seemed not to notice the cold. We took a turn or two around the garden; then Mr Tipper, taking up a position in the middle of the path, where the wind blew the keenest, said: 'I believe you have a fondness for Peckham, Mrs Pooter.'

I said, shivering: 'I have happy memories of Peckham, Mr Tipper, and should like to live there again one day.'

Mr Tipper said: 'Do you know, at all, where my sisters live, in Stonequarry Terrace? They have asked me to say that they would like to invite you there for luncheon one day.'

I said that I should be honoured. I often used to walk past Stonequarry Terrace, and a pleasant enough street it is – not unlike Brickfield Terrace, but without the railway. But I have never set foot in the Misses Tippers' house, our acquaintance in Peckham being confined to the Church and its Ladies' Quiet Hour Circle.

Mr Tipper said: 'I have what you may consider a curious proposal, Mrs Pooter. The fact is that my sisters have taken a great fancy to your house. I believe that the rents in Brickfield Terrace are much of a muchness with those in Stonequarry Terrace. Now, you have a mind to return to Peckham, Mrs Pooter, and they have a mind to come and live in Holloway. The proximity of the railway troubles them not; but I am given to understand that it vexes you greatly. The proposition I wish to put to you is this, Mrs Pooter. Should you take to my sisters' place, and all other things being equal, how would it be if you were to exchange houses?'

I was flabbergasted. Either the proposal was hare-brained, or it was a stroke of genius, I knew not which – and still know not which, as I pen these lines. I stammered: 'I can hardly take in what you say, Mr Tipper! You must give me time to think! And of course, I shall have to consult my husband.'

Mr Tipper said: 'See the house first, Mrs Pooter, and then should you wish the plan to go forward a stage further, pray allow me to lay it, in more detail, before Mr Pooter.'

I shall do as he suggests. Mr Tipper has a positive way with him, and if I agreed to pursue his mad proposal, I should much rather he spoke to Charlie than that I did.

We went indoors, when I was able to press him to half a cup of warm water before he left. I was relieved that Mr Tipper had seemed unaware that during the whole of our interview in the garden, the Griffin boys next door had been grimacing at us from their conservatory, pulling their ears and distending their mouths with their thumbs. I do not anticipate, however, that the Griffin nuisance would affect the Sisters Tipper, since they mistrust fresh air and never go out into the garden.

APRIL 27. Tomorrow, we are to go traipsing up to Muswell Hill for two o'clock dinner, to a Mr Edgar Finsworth's – a complete stranger, the uncle of a school friend whom Charlie chanced to 'bump into.' No question of *my* wishes being canvassed, oh, no! Charlie's friend beckons, and Charlie jumps; and *I* am to take this unknown friend, not to mention his unknown uncle, on trust, and give up my Sunday for the privilege of being in their company. Even had I put my foot down and refused to go, I should still be at the mercy of Charlie's other friends, who 'drop in' of a Sunday as of right. When it comes to *my* friends, then it is a different story – I 'see too much of them,' and they are 'too much of an influence' on me, or they 'put fanciful ideas into my head' and so on *ad infinitum,* every time Annie Fullers (now Mrs James, of Sutton) sets foot across the threshold, or I across hers. One day I shall acquaint Charlie in plain terms where lies the difference in quality between *my* friends and *his*.

Countermanded tomorrow's half-leg of mutton from the butcher's; but ordered a little scrag end with which to make Monday's 'mutton cakes.' Told Sarah (my maid) particularly, to make it plain to Mr Larkman, the butcher, that we shall be going out for dinner tomorrow, and that the scrag end is only for Monday supper.

APRIL 28. To Muswell Hill, to a house known as Watney Lodge, for two o'clock dinner. For once in our lives, instead of arriving an hour early, and having to walk about the streets, we arrived almost late, very flushed and out of breath. I never knew such a man as Charlie for not knowing how long it should take to get to a place. Usually, he will ask my opinion on the length of the journey; if I think half an hour, then I will say an hour, to be on the safe side; Charlie then takes my hour and extends it into two hours, to allow for unforeseen circumstances; and that is why we are always so early. As to this present occasion, I was preoccupied in adding up my household accounts, and so instead of doubling the time I thought it should take to Muswell Hill, I mistakenly halved it. For once, Charlie decided to accept my estimate at face value; and thus we only arrived in the nick of time.

We were greeted by a friendly collie, called Banjo, who very much reminded me of what Mrs Batch's dog, Claude, must be like when not suffering from melancholia. I must remember to ask after Claude when I take luncheon with the Misses Tipper. This is to be on Thursday week.

Whilst Mr Edgar Finsworth showed Charlie his family pictures, of which there were a great many, Mrs Finsworth took me upstairs to brush the paw marks off my new Bombay flannel skirt, and apply some common soap. They seemed an agreeable couple, although it struck me that they are somewhat elderly to be wanting to make the effort of giving hospitality to strangers. Of the nephew, Mr 'Teddy' Finsworth, Charlie's old school friend, to whom I had been briefly introduced downstairs, I had, and have, no impression – he seemed as colourless as a glass of water, not by any means the great 'swell' one would expect the Deputy Town Clerk of Middlesboro' (as he has risen to become) to be. By way of making conversation with Mrs Finsworth, I remarked that 'Teddy' Finsworth and Charlie's having bumped into one another, after all these years, was a case of 'the long arm of coincidence.'

Mrs Finsworth said: 'Not as long as you might think. We must have entertained just about his whole school to dinner by now.'

I said, startled: 'Does Mr Finsworth often come across his old school friends, then?'

Mrs Edgar Finsworth said: 'All the time. It is my belief that he goes out looking for them, whenever he comes to London. He makes a hobby of it, that's the size of it, Mrs Pooter. And if he cannot find any old school companions, then he will seek out those he used to share rooms with, or was in the church choir with, or once met on holiday, or anybody. And then he expects us to entertain them, at a few hours' notice. We were happy to do so in our younger days, but we are getting on now. I don't know why we have to put up with it, really I don't – present company excepted, of course.'

I was so awkward and embarrassed that I scarce listened to a word said to me all through dinner. Once I sensed that the gentleman on my right, a Mr Short, had spoken directly to me, and so I responded vivaciously: 'O, indeed!', whereupon he cried: 'See! Pooter! Mrs Pooter knows!' I did not know *what* I was supposed to know, and still do not. On the way home, Charlie told me that what Mr Short had said had been unfit for the ears of the Finsworths' dogs (they had another one, a spaniel called Bibbs, which licked all the blacking off Charlie's boots: that would be because I mix rancid dripping into the pot to make it go further), let alone ladies; and that I should not have replied.

Charlie also confided that whilst I had been closeted upstairs, he had had a very awkward time of it with Mr Edgar Finsworth, having unwittingly said 'the wrong thing' about most of his family portraits. I did not tell Charlie what an awkward time I had had of it with Mrs Edgar Finsworth.

APRIL 29. Writing to thank Mrs Edgar Finsworth for her hospitality yesterday, I added a wry PS: 'I well understand your fervent desire for Mr "Teddy" Finsworth to come across *fewer* of his old school friends. I would prefer that my husband came across *none* of his!' Only after I had posted the letter did it strike me that Mrs Finsworth might take this as a barb against her and her husband, which was certainly not intended, as they were very kind and attentive. After mature reflection, I penned another short note, explaining: 'It goes without saying, that I did not mean to imply that my husband and I were not honoured to be invited to your table – only that, with hindsight, we should not have allowed ourselves the pleasure of accepting.'

Having been denied the pleasure of Mr Cummings' and Mr Gowing's company yesterday, we were afforded it this evening, to make up for the omission. Charlie, despite the unanimous opinion of the company that there is nothing more uninteresting than another person's dreams, insisted upon regaling us with a long and desperate account of his latest nightmare, in which he encountered some huge blocks of ice, which proved to be on fire, whereupon he woke up bathed in perspiration.

I hope I have not been over-doing my supplications for a 'Wenham Lake' ice safe.

APRIL 30. *Pot Pourri: A Weekly Miscellany For Ladies* today publishes on its 'Cookery Notes' page, a recipe for Marlborough Peaches which has been taken almost word for word from *Lady Cartmell's Vade Mecum For the Bijou Household*. For this breathtaking example of plagiarism, one Mrs R. G. N., of Longramblington, Northumb., has been sent a halfcrown postal order. I have a good mind to write to the Editress.

Charlie still enjoys my 'mutton cakes,' but wonders if we need have them every week.

I return to Peckham and take luncheon with the Misses Tipper. Melancholy news of the dog Claude, mitigated by Mrs Batch's belief in the Happy Hunting Grounds. I am stunned by an invitation from Mr Franching, to meet Mr Hardfur Huttle. I see my first apparition. Pot Pourri has an important announcement.

20

MAY 7. *Pot Pourri: A Weekly Miscellany For Ladies* promises 'an important announcement which no reader should miss,' in its next number. I beg leave to doubt that this has any connexion with my recipe for 'mutton cakes.' I do not understand that journal: today they wasted a quarter of a page on a recipe for a common suet crust. I suppose that next, they will be instructing their readers upon how to mix cocoa.

He bowed perfunctorily

MAY 9. I have not set foot in Peckham since we left our dear little house in Shanks Place over a year ago. Alighting from the 'bus rather early for my luncheon engagement with the Misses Tipper, I took a turn as far as Lomax, the fruiterers', and back, for old times' sake. Shanks Place is meaner and narrower than I remembered it, and the house smaller, and I should not want to live in it now. But Peckham itself is 'a horse of a different colour'! How my heart ached to see the familiar shops, and familiar sights, and familiar faces! I saw Mr Sumpter, of the Peckham Harriers, going into the Metropolitan Tabernacle – he bowed perfunctorily, as if I had never left, and he still encountered me several times a month!

Stonequarry Terrace was just as I pictured it in memory's eye – the big house on the corner lending it a substantial air, whilst the May blossom in the little front gardens made everything look quite countrified. The Misses Tippers' residence, No. 14, boasts a yew tree in the front and another in the back – so that, without recourse to mendacity, it would be quite in order to call the house 'The Yews.' There are bow windows front and back – and *no railway*! Instead, the garden slopes gently down to the mellow old wall of Ackthorpe, Hollyman & Moxon's 'Jamboree Ales' Brewery.

We were just four for luncheon – the Misses Tippers' other guest being none other than their next-door neighbour Mrs Batch, a lady of the middle years who wore a black 'Ermyntrude' canvas cloth mantle trimmed with wool, Guipure lace and ribbon bows, which she would not take off, saying that she was a martyr to draughts and cold. I felt almost as if I knew Mrs Batch, being briefly acquainted with her dog; and so, in order to 'break the ice,' I expressed my hope that Claude was restored to canine good health and high spirits.

Mrs Batch, rolling her eyes and wringing her hands, cried: 'Ah! He has gone over!'

I was shocked at this news, and said I was ever so sorry to hear it.

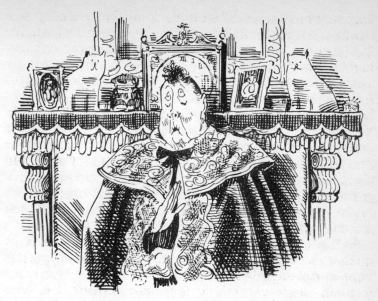

Mrs Batch, rolling her eyes and wringing her hands,
cried, 'Ah! He has gone over.'

Miss Tipper Jnr said, with a sigh: 'Our brother could do nothing for him. He was too far into his decline.'

Miss Tipper Senr said: 'He had to be put down. There was no other course.'

My recollection of Claude, poor animal, was that, although seedy and mopish, he had looked only as if it needed a powder or two to bring him back to the 'pink' of condition; but I imagine that Mr Tipper knows his business. Again I said how sorry I was, to hear of Claude's sad demise.

Mrs Batch said: 'Ah! But there is no need to be. *We are in touch!*'

Miss Tipper Jnr expanded: 'Claude speaks to Mrs Batch regularly.'

'Which he never did before,' added Miss Tipper Senr, nodding vigorously.

Mrs Batch explained: 'I go to a Medium, one Madame Doyle, who is the earthly instrument for Princess Crow Feather, of the Navaho nation. Claude speaks to me as often as is convenient for him, through Princess Crow Feather, from the Happy Hunting Grounds. He tells me that there is everything there that a dog could wish for, and that – ' (here Mrs Batch chuckled) ' – he spends the live-long day chasing rabbits!'

Charlie, were I to recount this conversation (but I must not, at this juncture, let him know that I have been to Peckham!) would undoubtedly snort and rejoin: 'Then the Happy Hunting Grounds cannot be so very happy for the rabbits!' I must say that the same thought passed through my own mind. I do not know whether I believe in Spiritualism or no. Years ago, I used to have séances with my then neighbour, Mrs Fussters, until Charlie put his foot down; but nothing came out of them. Perhaps Mrs Batch is more 'psychic' than I – or perhaps Madame Doyle, alias Princess Crow Feather, is 'pulling the wool over her eyes.'

I confined myself to a murmured conventionality to the effect that 'it must be a great solace to her,' and we went in to luncheon.

The dining room faces on the back, not on the street as does our breakfast parlour; and there is so little soot and smoke getting in, that the Misses Tipper could have their woodwork painted white, if they had a mind to. In the event it is chocolate-brown, the same as ours, but looking much cleaner. The Misses Tipper gave us an excellent kidney omelet, with some boiled and buttered sprouts, and custards in glasses to follow. I would not, myself, have served two 'eggy' dishes at the same table; but the meal was light and sensible. To drink, we had barley-water. The conversation rarely strayed far from the realm of Princess Crow Feather and the Happy Hunting Grounds. I was much interested at first, but ultimately I grew exasperated – especially when Mrs Batch clasped her hands and cried, as if in an ecstasy: 'Ah! And Claude is coming to visit me, you know! O, yes – he has promised!' She must be a very gullible woman.

As for the subject of Mr Oswald Tipper's 'little plan,' that, as was only to be expected, was never touched upon; but Miss Tipper Jnr, on the excuse to Mrs Batch that I was 'interested in rooms,' conducted me on a thorough tour of the establishment. I noticed a mouse-trap by the pantry door, and a tin of Sheen's 'Murderem' Cockroach Fumigating Fluid on a scullery shelf, but was otherwise favourably impressed. There was something of a malt smell coming up from the brewery, but both the Misses Tipper and Mrs Batch assured me that one hardly notices it after a while; and in any event, I found it quite pleasant.

Returning home at about four, I was altogether exhausted – doubtless from the excitement of seeing Peckham again. I lay down on the bed for a moment, and must have dozed off; for the next thing I knew, Charlie was bending over me, and about to burn a feather under my nose. I got up at once, feeling confused and guilty, as if he had 'caught me out' doing wrong – I know not why.

MAY 10. Awoke still feeling tired, but comfortable in the knowledge that there were no exhausting engagements to be fulfilled in the near future (or the distant future, come to that). If, at breakfast, I was dismayed to hear Charlie, who was brandishing a letter, announce that we are invited out to dinner this very evening, I was horror-struck to learn next that the invitation comes from none other than *Mr Franching of Peckham*! For, even as the name fell from Charlie's lips, I recalled what must have lain dormant in my memory for nigh on a year – that Mr Franching (as he revealed when he came to take 'pot luck' with us, and we had a long talk about Peckham) knows the Misses Tipper by sight, and also that he lives in a house known as 'Four Gables.' I cannot for the life of me understand why that name did not sear itself into my brain when I casually noticed it on a gate-post yesterday. *'Four Gables' is the big house on the corner of Stonequarry Terrace, but seven doors from the Misses Tipper!*

I said: 'We cannot possibly accept, at such short notice.'

Charlie said sharply: 'We must accept. It is to meet Mr Hardfur Huttle, the distinguished journalist, who has come all the way from America.'

I said: 'He has not come over especially.'

Charlie said even more sharply: 'Don't be silly, Carrie. Mr Franching does send his apologies for the short notice, but two intended guests have let him down. We cannot possibly disappoint him.'

There was to be no dissuading him from accepting – he had already started writing out the telegram.

I said: 'Very well, but you will have to buy me a new dress. The one I got for the Mansion House Ball is in tatters, and I have nothing to wear.'

Never have I derived so little enjoyment from buying a dress (it is in bottle green surah, with short puffed sleeves, pulled tight with smocking; and smocking at the waist and neck, which is scalloped), so apprehensive am I of the evening ahead. Whilst I am unlikely to encounter the Misses Tipper at Mr Franching's table – they hardly ever go out – I have no way of knowing how remote is the possibility of Mrs Batch being among those present – her interest in Spiritualism, if known to Mr Franching, could very well recommend itself as a subject to amuse an American. What I am more afraid of is that among the guests there could easily be someone – Mr Franching himself, even! – who might have noticed me in the vicinity of 'Four Gables' yesterday (for, being still early upon reaching the Misses Tippers', I walked several times around a rectangle described by Stonequarry Terrace, Schools Lane, Brewery Street and Hornby Road). What am I to say if my neighbour at dinner addresses me thus: 'And did you enjoy your walk yesterday, Mrs Pooter? Little did I know, as you passed by my window three or four times, that I should have the honour of sitting next to you this evening, and assisting you to potatoes!'? The supposition does not bear thinking about.

I worried to such a degree that I brought on a sick headache, and had to lie down again, this time with a compress. I did not allow myself to entertain hopes that, out of pity and concern for his wife, Charlie's resolve to go out tonight would falter. He is a man of iron, once he has set himself upon a certain course.

Later: I write these lines in a rhapsody of excitement, at what has come to pass this night. I can hardly bring myself to believe it – indeed, there is a part of me that does not *wish* to believe it – and I must pinch myself from time to time, as an assurance that I am not dreaming.

Withal, I must continue my impressions of this eventful day in their proper chronological order. To begin with: my fears that my 'Peckham adventure' (as I shall call it!) should be exposed, proved to be groundless, as I ought to have known that they would. Mr Franching is not of the calibre to be influenced or restricted by the accident of geographical proximity in the selection of his friends; therefore, the company, which was large (and attended by a hired waiter), was drawn from every quarter of the Metropolis. Even had another resident of

*Charlie was obliged to press his shirt front
into service as a pencil-jotter*

Stonequarry Terrace chanced to have been present – and that would have been by virtue of that person's intrinsic worth *and that alone* – then I cannot imagine any topic so drab and mundane as my perambulations about the neighbourhood, being thought worthy of remark: the evening was on far too lofty a plane for that. There was a *menu* card at each place; we passed our cards around the table and wrote our names on them; and mine shall go in my plush-covered album.

Mr Hardfur Huttle, the guest of honour, is a dominating – I will not say domineering – personage, who seized command of Mr Franching's table at once, as a captain takes the wheel, and steered our discourse as he pleased. He said so many witty or controversial things, some profound, others plain rude or silly, that Charlie was kept scribbling on his shirt cuffs all the way from Peckham to London Bridge before Mr Huttle's *mots* went out of his head; and on the 'last lap' to Holloway, was obliged to press his shirt-front into service as a pencil-jotter. Since these notes are bound to be transcribed in my husband's diary, I will forbear from using up my precious space on Mr Huttle's table-talk, save for two examples.

Apropos of some comments he had made to the company at large, on the subject of the electric light, I ventured to ask him: 'And Mr Huttle, what is your opinion of the ice safe, which I have been told is the coming thing?'   ·

This was Mr Huttle's reply: 'What is my opinion of tap water, madam? What is my opinion of this knife and fork? Why do we eat at table, and not on the floor? To what end does Mr Franching equip his domicile with a roof, and walls, and doors, and windows? Anyone who is told that the ice safe is the coming thing, madam, has the right to ask: "If it is only now coming, why was it not here before?" '

By and by, I shall remind Charlie of that speech.

Later on, I had the opportunity to ask Mr Huttle his opinion of Peckham, as a place to live. Mr Huttle, who in some ways reminds me of Lupin, replied as follcws: 'Peckham is, madam, as ancient Athens was. Within our host's fair suburb we have all that civilised man requires. Peckham is a seat of learning, a temple of thought, a basilica of culture and a citadel of truth. Peckham is not across the river from London – London is across the river from Peckham. The best talk is to be found in Peckham, the finest brains are to be found in Peckham, the most incandescent wit is to be found in Peckham. And how do I know, madam? *Because we are here!*'

I shall remind Charlie of that, also.

Brilliant though it was, the conversation – recitation, I almost wrote – of Mr Hardfur Huttle was, so far as *I* was concerned, to be but a mere curtain-raiser to this most memorable of evenings. Taking our leave of our host and his distinguished guest of honour, we walked along Stonequarry Terrace towards the road that would take us down to the station. The Misses Tippers' house was in darkness, as was only to be expected – thcy do not sit up late: indeed, their house had been in darkness when we arrived at Mr Franching's for dinner. But despite the hour, lights still glowed in the windows of No. 16, the residence of Mrs Batch. Recalling this lady's long exposition upon the messages she receives from her dog Claude in the Happy Hunting Grounds, I wondered if she were perhaps closeted in a seance with Princess Crow Feather – I believe midnight is reckoned to be a particularly appropriate time for calling up the spirits. Possibly (I allowed myself to speculate with irreverent amusement), Mrs Batch had had word from the Other World that Claude was about to pay his promised visit, and was waiting up for him!

As we passed No 16, Charlie implored me to hurry, lest we miss our train. Hurry we did; yet I saw as much as had we dawdled; and every detail of the scene is etched on my memory. The curtains of Mrs Batch's drawing room were undrawn. The gas was brightly lit, so that the lace blinds were as rice paper – one could

see straight through them. Mrs Batch was sitting in a
rocking chair, rocking backwards and forwards, and
laughing, or crying, copiously – either, or both. My
hand trembles at what I am about to write next. Mrs
Batch's dog Claude, as he unmistakably was, and who is
known to me to have passed over in Holloway three
months ago, *was sitting in the window as large as life,
and wagging his tail!*

My husband takes another day off. He is discouraging on the subject of Peckham. Lupin loses his position — only to gain a superior one. Mr Tipper calls inconveniently.

21

MAY 11. For only the second time in his life – and the first in twenty years – Charlie would not get up to go to business today. His belief is that he was suffering from lobster poisoning. My belief is that it was champagne poisoning, the same as it was on the other occasion. Charlie protested: 'I drank very little of Mr Franching's champagne.' I said: 'Then the lobster must have drunk it.' Took him up some toast-and-water at noon. By six o'clock he was feeling recovered enough to fancy 'just some of the calf's head we were going to have last night, if we hadn't gone out; with perhaps a little asparagus and a bite of apricot-jam lattice tart.' He got an invalid cutlet and a plate of arrowroot *blanc-mange*.

The laundress brought back the cuffs and shirt front which she took away first thing, saying that 'she 'ad just noticed they 'ad writing all over them.' Unthinkingly, I told her that the writing was done with (only later realising that Charlie cannot have entered up his diary yet, and that now he will have to record Mr Hardfur Huttle's talk from memory). The laundress said: 'That don't make no diff'rence, mum. I came back to warn you that written-on cuffs is a penny hextra.'

MAY 12. It being as fine a Sunday afternoon as we have had since last summer, I prevailed upon Charlie to come for a walk. I led him down some of the meanest and dustiest streets in Holloway – in which stratagem I had a purpose! After prompting Charlie to recollect some of the things said by Mr Hardfur Huttle, and getting him to admit that he is 'a wonderfully brilliant man, if a dangerous one,' I asked at length: 'And what do you say to his dissertation on the delights of Peckham?'

Charlie said: 'O, that was "tosh." '

I said: 'When *I* said, on the way home, that Mr Huttle came out with a lot of nonsense, you said I didn't have the intellect to form an opinion one way or the other.'

Charlie said: 'There is no need to sound so injured, my dear – I freely admit that some of Mr Huttle's clever allusions went even over *my* head. When I said just now that he was speaking "tosh" in that one regard of Peckham, however, you must appreciate that he was doing so quite wittingly. He expressed himself in such extravagant and lavish terms only to "butter up" his host. It is the American idea of politeness.'

I said: 'Then, after all, he doesn't care for Peckham?'

Charlie said: 'I didn't say that.'

I said: 'I should think not, indeed. Why – look at this thoroughfare we are walking along, and compare it with any street in Peckham!'

Charlie said: 'I concur with you, Carrie, that the wall of the female penitentiary is not the most pleasing of vistas; nor can I imagine why you have brought us this way.'

I said: 'If we still lived in Peckham, we should be strolling about the Rye.'

Charlie said: 'But we do *not* still live in Peckham, and thankful am I that we do not! Ugh! What an age it takes to get there! Whatever possessed us to live so far off?'

It is a long row that I have to hoe.

MAY 13. Calamitous tidings – or, as I shall say, tidings which at first seemed calamitious, yet upon mature reflection seem less so. Lupin is discharged from Mr Perkupp's employ. It appears that he has been so remiss as to recommend to one of the firm's most valued clients, Mr Crowbillon, who was dissatisfied with what he has been getting from Perkupp's, that he should take his business to the firm of Messrs Gylterson, Sons & Co Ltd, who (so Lupin avers: I know nothing of such things) are more 'go-ahead.' Charlie regards this as an act of treachery. I said, in Lupin's defence: 'Treachery against whom? Certainly not Mr Crowbillon, if he benefits from Lupin's advice.' Charlie fulminated: 'The name of Pooter will be blackened from one end of the Square Mile to the other! By this action, our son has lost Mr Perkupp his best customer!' I said: 'No! By *his own* actions, or the lack of them, *Mr Perkupp* has lost his best customer. By *Lupin's* action, Glyterson, Sons and Co have gained a new client. Therefore, the name of Pooter is certainly not blackened in *their* quarter of the Square Mile!' Charlie said: 'You do not understand, Carrie.' Nor do I: but having 'stood up' for Lupin made me feel less mortified than I might have been; and when Lupin himself came home, he was so cheerful and uncaring that I came to the view that Charlie is making a mountain out of a molehill, and that the situation might have been considerably worse. Mr Perkupp could have visited his wrath upon Charlie, for having insinuated Lupin into his office in the first place; and then where should we have been? I did not muse thus aloud, since I did not think it would comfort Charlie.

I was surprised to see Lupin wearing one of Posh's 'three-shilling' hats; for I thought he would sooner walk the streets bareheaded, than wear any thing associated with his one-time arch-rival in love, the husband of Daisy Mutlar. But no, I am wrong: Lupin and he are the greatest of friends again. If I do not understand the ways of the City, as Charlie tells me I do not, even less do I understand the ways of the young.

MAY 14. *Pot Pourri: A Weekly Miscellany For Ladies* announces — taking up the whole of what is normally the 'Cookery Notes' page to do so — that owing to its unequalled and unprecedented success, particularly amongst lovers of 'the great outdoors,' and 'the active woman,' the journal is to be amalgamated with *The Lady Bicyclist*, commencing next week. I shall not subscribe.

Charlie had leave from Mr Perkupp to stay at home this morning, having been told off to write a letter to Mr Crowbillon, apologising for the 'foolish advice' given to him by 'an inexperienced clerk' (as he is to describe his only son!). Much good that will do. Lupin, having nothing to do until mid-day, when he was going off to have luncheon in the City with Mr Murray Posh, was also at home, where he devoted most of the morning to throwing an apple up in the air and catching it in his new hat. In consequence, with both my menfolk in the house, Mr Oswald Tipper could scarcely have chosen a more unpropitious morning to call, which he explained he had ventured to do, seeing that he had been in the next street attending to a grey parrot. Fortunately, I was just passing through the hall at the very moment that Sarah (my maid) opened the door.

I said in a low voice: 'I am sorry, but I cannot receive you, Mr Tipper, as my husband and son are in the house, and they know nothing of our business yet.'

Mr Tipper whispered: 'Did you form a favourable impression of my sisters' house – that is all I came to ask?'

I said: 'Yes, but we cannot discuss it on the doorstep. You must go now.'

When I went back into the parlour, Charlie asked: 'Who was that at the door?'

I said: 'Only the knife-grinder.'

He said: 'At the front? What are we coming to?'

Lupin, who was standing by the window, said: 'He looked quite a "swell" for a knife-grinder.'

I said: 'Perhaps that is why he came to the front door.'

Should I dare to proceed any further with the audacious plan to exchange houses with the Misses Tipper, then it is inevitable that Mr Tipper and Lupin should meet, when I shall have some explaining to do. As the poet truly wrote: 'O, what a tangled web we weave, when first we practise to deceive!'

MAY 15. Intended to broach the subject of Peckham with Charlie, but only in the most general terms – just so that when Mr Oswald Tipper comes to speak to him, it will not fall like 'a bolt from the blue.' However, after reading the letter that came for him this evening, he was in no mood for discussion upon this, or any other, topic. The letter was from Mr Crowbillon, and it was to the effect that far from the 'inexperienced clerk' having given him 'foolish advice,' his transferring of his affairs to Messrs Gylterson, Sons & Co Ltd was the best day's work he had done in many years. Charlie sat in a trance, repeating over and over again, in a variety of intonations: 'What will Mr Perkupp say? What will Mr Perkupp say? What will Mr Perkupp say?'

There was also a letter in the evening post for Lupin. Shortly before supper, whilst I was in the kitchen, making a German sauce (Sarah, my maid, always lets the eggs curdle), he came down and tossed his letter on the table.

Lupin said: 'The guv seems awfully "blue" this evening, and I know he's still in a "wax" with me. See here, ma – d'you think I should show him this?'

'This' was from Messrs Gylterson, Sons & Co Ltd, offering Lupin Pooter, Esquire, an appointment in their office at no less than £200 per annum, and a commission for any new clients introduced by him!

I cried, holding back my tears: 'O, Willie – Lupin, I should say! You are another Hardfur Huttle!'

Lupin said: 'Hulloh! And my aunt has a brother in Portugal!' – one of his mystifying expressions, meaning, I supposed, that he did not comprehend me.

Kissing my clever son, I said: 'Never mind. Show this to your father you must – but tomorrow!'

Mr Oswald Tipper's fears of shilly-shallying. My Powers. Sarah (my maid) proves an ally in my campaign to get to Peckham. A week of rewarding séances, disrupted by the absurd Mr Gowing. Matrimonial disharmony, engendered by the same gentleman. The Misses Tipper make a confession.

22

MAY 17. Called upon Mr Oswald Tipper at his consulting rooms. Receiving me, Mr Tipper said: 'But Mrs Pooter, where is your little cat?'

I said: 'I have not come about the cat, Mr Tipper. I am here about your proposition.'

Mr Tipper said: 'Alas! You know my rule, Mrs Pooter, as to mixing personal and professional business. May I call on you this afternoon?'

I said, in no little exasperation: 'No, you may not, as my son will be at home. What are we to do, Mr Tipper – meet in the street?'

This satirical shaft evidently suggested a compromise to Mr Tipper, for, divesting himself of his overall, he accompanied me out into the hall. At his front door (I had come in by the side, where his waiting room is), he said: 'If you are seriously considering the plan, Mrs Pooter, I would take it as a favour if you would write to my sisters, as an earnest that they may allow themselves hopes of a removal to Brickfield Terrace. You know how they are: they are both of a highly nervous and appre-hensive disposition; I would not wish to commit you further until we can be tolerably sure that, when they see the likelihood of their aspiration translating into reality, they will not take fright and commence to shilly-shally.'

I could hear my heart thumping madly as I said: 'No, we should not want *that*!' I agreed to do as Mr Tipper suggested; and this evening wrote to the Misses Tipper, although in the most guarded and circumspect terms, expressing my continuing interest in what their brother has proposed.

MAY 18. Lupin has taken to using bay rum again. He also, when he goes out at night, sports a buttonhole – that is, when he is not wearing evening dress. I expect we shall be vouchsafed the lady's name, in due course.

MAY 20. A letter from Miss Tipper Jnr, acknowledging mine of the 17th inst., but confessing herself unable to make out whether I wished to proceed any further with her brother's plan or no. The sisters Tipper are off to Royal Tunbridge Wells for two or three weeks, to take the waters; following upon which, they hope I will allow them to give themselves the pleasure of calling.

MAY 26. Until this day, not to a living soul have I imparted one word about the apparition of Claude, the collie dog, which I saw in the window of Mrs Batch's house on that fateful midnight. This evening, however, found us at Sutton for an informal supper (how I wish that Charlie would not call it 'meat-tea'!) with the James'; and no sooner had Annie Fullers (now Mrs James) led me upstairs to take off my bonnet, than, knowing her interest in such matters, I poured out everything, embellishing nothing, but leaving nothing out.

Annie was thrilled by my account. Keenly and eagerly did she ply me with questions. The principal one of these was: 'Did your husband sense Claude's presence?'

I replied: 'He cannot have done, Annie, or he would surely have remarked on it. A large dog, sitting in a lighted window at midnight and wagging its tail, would be bound to excite comment, even were it a thing of flesh and blood.'

Annie said: '*That*, you may rest assured, it was not! You are possessed of Powers, Carrie. I always sensed that you might be gifted in that way, even when we were at school.'

I said: 'I had no Powers when I used to sit with old Mrs Fussters.'

Annie said: 'Then she must have been a negative 'fluence. When you sit with *me*, dear Carrie, you will find me a positive 'fluence. I can't begin to tell you, what has not been revealed to me from the Other Side, since I took up table-turning again. You do know that I am now a professional medium?'

Of course, I knew nothing of the kind – I cannot keep up with Annie's pursuits and pastimes. Nor, as it proved, is she any such thing. Her interest in making up Japanese paper insects and the like having waned somewhat, she has taken to occupying a few of her afternoons in holding séances at the homes of a select number of acquaintances, who may express their appreciation of her labours with a small donation, discreetly presented, in a sealed envelope; and that is the size of it. This I was mightily relieved to hear; for until Annie elaborated on her latest enterprise, I had an unseemly vision of her sitting in a booth, with a kerchief tied around her head, on the jetty at Margate!

Mr James having to go down to Bristol, where the 'Cocee' or 'Coffoa' manufactory in which he now has an interest is established, Annie is to come up and stay with us for a few days, when we shall try some table-turning and hope to call up the spirits. In the interim, she has lent me a most fascinating book, called *There Is No Birth*, by Florence Singleyet, which she promises will change my life, as it has changed hers.

MAY 29. Sarah (my maid) came formally into the parlour this afternoon, to ask if she might take her week's holiday in September, instead of June as usual; as she and her sister would like to go to Clacton-on-Sea, where their Aunt Minnie lives, who will give them favourable terms; but they have not as yet got enough money put by. I told her that of course she might, adding: 'And how is your sister, Sarah? Is she still living at The Borough?'

Sarah confirmed that she was, 'seeing as 'ow it suited

211

'er, being 'andy for the match factory where she works.'

I said: 'It must be quite a journey for you, when you go to stay at Edith's lodgings. Wasn't The Borough easier to get to from Peckham?'

Sarah agreed that it was – much; and then, without any prompting from me, she volunteered the fierce rider: '*An' I wish we was back there, straight!*'

I have an ally in the house. I tipped Sarah a shilling, for her holiday fund.

MAY 30. Annie Fullers (now Mrs James, of Sutton) came to stay, much to Charles' displeasure. He has become so marked in his disapproval of my friendship with Annie, that at last I did what I have long promised myself to do, and told my husband some home truths about his own choice of friends. Perhaps I was more stinging in my rebuke than I ought to have been; at any rate, Charles all but openly quarrelled with Annie, being so withering in his contempt for things he does not understand (i.e., Spiritualism), that she was forced to defend herself, and he retreated with his tail between his legs.

Despite my husband's surly behaviour, I am sorry for a remark which I allowed myself to pass to Annie when he had gone. It was only because I wanted to appease Charlie's rudeness, but I should have held my tongue.

The remark was: 'There are times when I wish I had married Jerome Halfmoney.' This was disloyal, and untrue. I do *not* ever wish I had married Jerome Halfmoney – indeed, until today, I had not thought about him for years. It is just that occasionally I wish Charlie had something of the intellect of his sometime rival – the most towering and impressive First Lord of the Treasury that the Peckham Mock Parliament has ever had (so said the obituary notice by 'Brutus' in the *Camberwell Free Press*. Jerome Halfmoney died tragically young, of a fish-bone in the throat, leaving a wife and seven children).

Annie and I had no sooner made the preparations for a séance, than Mr Cummings arrived, closely followed

212

by Mr Gowing. It was a wonder their ears were not burning, after what I had said about them! Mr Cummings surprised me by expressing a sane interest in Spiritualism, and so we allowed him to join the circle. Mr Gowing also expressed an interest, but a vulgar one. Charlie took him off to sit in the kitchen, where we could hear them guffawing and sniggering. This coarse exhibition quite spoiled the atmosphere, and so put off 'Lina' (Annie's spirit) that she refused to 'come through.' The table did, however, tilt slightly towards all three of us in turn – or we each, comparing notes, felt that it had. Annie explained: 'Lina is telling us that she does not hold us responsible.' When I scolded Charlie in the privacy of our bedroom, he protested that it had been Mr Gowing who had done all the chortling that we could hear. I said: 'Then at what was he laughing, pray – his own witty sallies, or yours?' I considered this quite a shrewd retort, and I could tell that it had hit home.

MAY 31. Charlie spent a considerable amount of time concocting a satirical letter to the laundress, concerning her latest shortcomings. He was so pleased with his composition, which he read over many times with a smirk on his face, that I had not the heart to tell him that the laundress cannot read.

More table-turning this evening – Mr Cummings joined us and was again most sensible. Were it not for the inevitability of Mr Gowing trailing in his wake, Mr Cummings' visit could be almost tolerable – if only there were fewer of them. I still wonder why Mrs Cummings lets him out of the house so much. He is dull, but if every dull husband were turned out in the evenings, the streets would be jam-packed.

Tonight's séance was quite eventful. Annie went into a light trance, and then the table tilted towards me, and spelled out the letters L-S-D.

Mr Cummings whispered: 'Evidently something to do with money!'

Through Annie, the spirit 'Lina' then said, in a quaver-

213

ing voice: 'Not the whole!' In a flash, I understood what was being said to me: *Jerome Halfmoney*!

Again the table tilted towards me, this time quite violently. Mr Cummings said: 'It wants you to ask a question.' I knew that very well; but what question was I to ask of Jerome Halfmoney, with Mr Cummings present to relay every word that passed between us back to my husband? I said, trembling: 'I have no question.' Annie let out a moan, and then slumped forward on the table, as if in a deep sleep. Presently she shook her head and came out of her trance, uttering dreamily: 'I have been somewhere wondrous!' She could not, or would not, expand on that exclamation.

Now Annie knows all about Jerome Halfmoney of course; and it was only yesterday that his name passed my lips in her presence. Yet even – and I banish the very thought as base – were my dear friend capable of trickery, which in any case could avail her nothing, there was too much that was inexplicable – mysterious thuds, a lighted coal dropping without warning into the hearth, and so on and so on – to allow of the possibility of deception. What is more likely is that by saying the rash thing that I did to Annie about Jerome Halfmoney, I disturbed his spirit and thus unwittingly 'called him up.'

As a married woman, I do not feel that any further intercourse with Mr Halfmoney's spirit would be proper – not even in the interest of psychic experiment. I shall try to prevail upon Charlie to sit with us tomorrow. Jerome Halfmoney was a gentleman, and I am sure that his spirit is one too. It would not wish to embarrass a lady by its attentions, when her husband was present.

JUNE 1. Charlie consented to join the séance, and seemed quite impressed when the table spelled out C-A-T for him. He surmised that this might be in reference to his Aunt Maggie, whose second name – so he now says – was Catherine. This I find far-fetched. My own explanation is that the spirits' simple message to the 'greenhorn' at our table, was as a rag-book is to a child that is

214

learning to read. At all events, Charlie was sufficiently encouraged to say that he would sit at our next séance. Perhaps he will then he entrusted with a longer word.

JUNE 2. No séance today, it being Sunday. Annie went over to Kensington, to visit her mother; whilst Lupin – much to the disgust of Charlie, who finds something improper in such an arrangement – has gone to stay with his friends the Murray Poshes for a few days. I don't know whether Charlie would be less or more agitated were he to be made aware (as I have been, thanks to the sharp eyes of Annie, an avid reader of 'Mr Tittle-Tattle's Corner' in *The Theatregoer*) that Mr Murray Posh has a sister; also that Lupin has taken with him a whole pint bottle of bay rum, as well as his evening clothes.

After the excitements of the past week, and with only the two of us, it was rather a dull day – quite like old times, in fact.

JUNE 3. Our séance this evening was rendered a farce by the presence at it of Mr Gowing, who kept up a stream of cheap jokes and silly remarks. That man would sing comic songs at a funeral tea – he has no sense of occasion whatsoever. Despite his imbecilities, 'Lina' had much to say to us. Mrs James was given the name of a Captain Drinkwater, a very old friend of her father's, who has been dead some years; whilst I had the message that 'NIPUL (that is, Lupin, spelled backwards) will be very rich.' This I found quite upsetting, I know not why – I should have had something to be upset about had 'Lina' informed me that Lupin will be very poor! There was also something about Lupin and Mrs – *or was it Miss?* – Posh, but Mr Gowing was clowning so much that I could not make head nor tail of it. Charlie has promised me that he will not allow Mr Gowing at our last séance tomorrow. I have promised Charlie that if he does, I shall pack my bags and accompany Annie back to Sutton.

*Our séance this evening was rendered a farce by
the presence at it of Mr Gowing*

JUNE 4. Only Mr Gowing could contrive to disrupt an
evening as much by his absence as by his presence.
Whilst he positively did *not* attend the séance, the
uproar was such that he might as well have done. Before
we sat at the table, Mr Gowing brought round a sealed
envelope containing a question. He said he would not
stop (he had not been invited to), but that if the spirits
could answer his question, then he would believe in
Spiritualism. For myself, I do not care a fig whether Mr
Gowing chooses to believe in spiritualism or in the flat
earth theory; but Annie, unwisely, accepted his chal-
lenge, and gave the question to 'Lina.' Needless to say, it
was a jape: what Mr Gowing had written was: '*What's
old Pooter's age?*' Charlie – of whose wholehearted
conversion to Spiritualism I was beginning to entertain
high hopes – at once fell into a towering rage, rounding
not on the absent culprit, but on Annie, for bringing 'this
nonsense' into the house! I have never seen him like it: I
thought he was about to forbid her ever to darken our
doorstep again. Indeed, when we were alone, he
revealed to me – still fulminating – how closely he had
come to it.

216

Charlie said: 'If I could be certain that your friend Mrs James called me a particular kind of fool, as I hope I am mistaken in thinking that she did, then she would never enter this house again.'

I said: 'If Annie did say such a thing, in the heat of the moment, and under the extreme provocation of the insulting things which *you* flung at *her*, then she would have been justified, for you *are* a particular kind of fool!'

Charles protested: 'Caroline!'

I said: 'I am sorry, Charles, but *only* a fool would stare Truth in the face and call it nonsense!'

Charles sneered: 'What truth, pray?'

I said: 'The truth that there are those to whom is vouchsafed a glimpse beneath the Veil.'

Charles scoffed: 'Pah!'

I said calmly: 'You may "pah!" until you are blue in the face. If I told you that I have myself seen, with my own eyes, an apparition from the Other Side, as plainly as I see you now, what would you say to that?'

Charles said: 'I should say that you were mistaken, or deranged.'

I said, with simple dignity: 'Then I agree with every word that Annie uttered. Pray leave this room.'

It was the worst quarrel we have ever had.

JUNE 11. Charlie and I have barely spoken to one another for a week. Today, thinking to make the peace, I said, referring to Lucy Onions, the woman who made some of my cushions, whom I have not set eyes on for months, until this morning I espied her going into a pawnshop: 'Guess whom I saw today?'

Charles sneered: 'The Ghost of Christmas Past, I shouldn't wonder!'

It will be another week before I speak to him again.

JUNE 12. The Misses Tipper called, refreshed from their sojourn at Royal Tunbridge Wells. Notwithstanding their brother's fears that they would shilly-shally, the sisters were most positive in their desire to exchange houses – more positive, indeed, than I discovered myself to be, upon observing Miss Tipper Jnr produce a tape-measure, with which she proceeded to measure the curtains. It is not that I would not dearly love to live in Peckham again — the house in Stonequarry Terrace is one after my own heart: but the prospect of preparing Charlie for a visit from Mr Oswald Tipper is a daunting one. I frankly acquainted the Misses Tipper with my position; whereupon Miss Tipper Senr took it upon herself to remark: 'A wife's fear of her husband is understandable, Mrs Pooter. That is why we urge you to leave all the arrangements to Oswald.' I replied haughtily: 'Forgive me, Miss Tipper, but I have no fear of my husband. I am grateful to Mr Tipper for his good offices, but until I have found an opportune moment to apprise Mr Pooter of what we are about, there is nothing more to be done.'

Tea was brought in. To change the subject, and because I knew that my tale would be of interest to them, I related to the Misses Tipper how I had seen the apparition of the dog Claude in Mrs Batch's window. The effect of my words was astounding. Miss Tipper Senr began to weep and moan; whilst Miss Tipper Jnr, with pursed lips, went over to the door, and opened it, and looked about, as if to see if there might be anybody at the keyhole; and then returned to her chair. She then commenced the following strange narrative.

'Mrs Pooter, what I have to tell you must not go beyond these four walls. *What you saw was no apparition*. Claude was not put down at our brother's, as we were regrettably forced to pretend.'

Miss Tipper Senr wailed: 'We lost him!'

Miss Tipper Jnr said: '*I* will tell the story, Amelia. Whilst we were walking the dog from your house to Carthby Terrace, Mrs Pooter, on the day we were taking him to Oswald's on Mrs Batch's behalf, he slipped out of his lead and ran after a brewer's dray. The smell of beer has always excited him. He goes mad when the wind blows up through the "Jamboree Ales" brewery into Stonequary Terrace.

218

'He had been listless as you know, Mrs Pooter, and this sudden burst of energy took us by surprise. We are neither of us as young as we were, and we could not catch up with him. He raced off down the Holloway Road, and that was the last that we saw of him.'

'Until he came back!' sobbed Miss Tipper Senr.

Miss Tipper Jnr continued: 'We were distraught. You may imagine our position. We had failed our friend Mrs Batch, as custodians of her dog. We *had* to let her believe he had been put down; to have told her the truth would have been to nourish hopes of his ultimate return, and that would have been cruel. There was no telltale address on his collar, and so there seemed no possibility that she would ever see him again, and our compassionate deception be exposed.

'O, Mrs Pooter, would that we had listened more to Oswald, when he was a student at the Royal Veterinary College! With how many stories did he not regale us, of dogs which have walked hundreds – nay! thousands! – of miles to restore themselves to the bosoms of their masters; relying only upon their own unfathomable instincts to find their way home! To a dog, what is the distance between Holloway and Peckham? It is nothing!'

Although disappointed at so mundane an explanation of my 'vision,' I was naturally pleased for Mrs Batch. I said: 'And so Claude and his mistress were re-united. She must have been in a transport of delight!'

Miss Tipper Jnr said: 'We know nothing of Mrs Batch's sensations in respect of the dog's return, since she will no longer speak to us. Nor will our other neighbours, who appear to believe either that we gave away the dog, or worse, sold him, whilst he was in our charge.'

Miss Tipper placed her hands together in an imploring gesture, and moaned: 'So now you understand, Mrs Pooter – *it is more imperative than ever that we expedite our removal from Stonequarry Terrace!*'

*An unwarranted intrusion by the railway company.
We dine at Lupin's new apartments, and meet his pro-
spective fiancée. Charlie does some nocturnal
business.*

23

JUNE 24. It is the last straw. Today two men in bowler hats, officers of the Great Northern Railway, came to the door and asked leave to walk down the garden, to inspect the line. To my enquiry as to what they were about, they revealed that the Company intends to put a semaphore signal there, connecting with the signal-box at the coal yards.

I said: 'Does this mean that trains will be stopping outside my back door?'

One of the men said, with a fruity chuckle: 'They had better do, ma'am, or the driver will find himself in trouble!'

The other one, who seemed more to comprehend my distress, said in a kindly manner: 'The signal pole will be on the railway embankment, not in your garden, ma'am; but since the semaphore will over-hang your wall to ever such a slight degree, the Company will agree to paying a peppercorn rent.'

The men were all afternoon measuring up, and had only just gone when Charlie came home. I had spilled out the news before he had time even to take his hat off.

Charlie said airily: 'O, yes, I had a letter about the matter from the landlord. I would have told you, but you were in one of your sulks.'

I said: 'I do *not* sulk, Charles; and what do you intend to do about it?'

Charlie said: 'There is nothing *to* be done about it. They are allowed by Act of Parliament to put up the signal, provided that they pay a peppercorn rent.'

I said: 'I do not care twopence for their peppercorn rent!'

Charlie said: 'I expect that *twopence* is all it will be!' He then laughed immoderately.

There is no trouble so great that he will not make a jest of it. I said: 'I suppose you would let them build a locomotive shed at the bottom of the garden, if they paid a peppercorn rent! What about the trains stopping, and all the passengers staring into my windows?'

Charles said: 'We are assured that the trains will not usually be stopping – only on particular days, at particular times, when there is congestion up the line.'

I said: 'O, I see! Then our privacy is to be at the mercy of *Bradshaw*, is it? I am sick of this house, Charles, and I want to leave it!'

Charles said: 'Nonsense, dear! We have had some of the happiest days of our marriage here!' Try as I may. I could not bring myself to say another word, my heart was pounding so.

Perhaps I might go and stay with Annie Fullers (now Mrs James), at Sutton, for a few days, telling him that my nerves are suffering; and then I could write him a letter, proposing the exchange of houses with the Misses Tipper.

JUNE 29. The new semaphore signal was put up today. Lupin took one look at it and announced that he intends to leave home. He proposes to take rooms in Bayswater, near his friends, Mr and Mrs Murray Posh. He will have to pay two guineas a week; but as Lupin says, it is worth it, to be at a good address.

I will admit that no trains have stopped at the bottom of our garden yet; but they do positively *slow down* as they approach the signal. I shall either have to order thicker blinds for all the back rooms; or give Charlie an ultimatum that I must leave here – with him or without him.

JULY 1. It is very sad to lose Lupin. His room looks so

forlorn with all his things gone; but it is not as if he is off to the far ends of the earth, as when he took up his position with Throstle & Epps' Linen Bank. His father still professing not to understand why he wants to go to Bayswater, Lupin said that Brickfield Terrace was 'a bit off' – with which verdict I heartily concur! Charlie said: 'The neighbourhood has always been good enough for your parents, my boy.' I said: 'Nonsense, dear. We had rooms here when we were first married, only because we could not afford to live anywhere else; and as soon as you had made something of yourself, we were off to Peckham like a shot! Why you wanted to come back, I shall never know.' Lupin said: 'The mater's "hit it," guv. Besides, it is not a question of being good or bad. There is no money in this dump, and I am not going to rot away my life in the suburbs.' I wish he had not made that disparaging remark about the suburbs; for I had been on the verge of recommending a return to Peckham, in the hope that Lupin would back me up.

JULY 2. A letter came for me from Mr Oswald Tipper. I told Charlie that it was from Miss Jibbons, enquiring whether I should require anything to be made in the way of holiday clothes this year (we are off to 'good old' Broadstairs again!); and subsequently burned it. The letter read: 'My dear Madam, This is intended only as a reminder that, should you have any need of my services in the execution of the business we have discussed – and upon which my sisters are *most anxious* to proceed, as expeditiously as is possible – then I am at your disposal. I have the honour to be, my dear Madam, &c &c &c.'

JULY 3. Charlie in a state of high excitement because Lupin came with Mrs Murray Posh to see us, in a trap driven by Mrs Posh. One would think they had eloped, the way Charlie carried on after they had left! If he said: 'Did you hear how he kept calling her "Daisy"?' once, he must have said it a dozen times. Charlie makes not the slightest effort to accommodate to modernity – it is not all that long ago since he ceased to grumble because Lupin does not 'Sir' him any more!

Besides, if he believes there is anything indecorous in Lupin's friendship with Mrs Posh, why does he suppose that when we go to eight o'clock dinner at Lupin's new apartments tomorrow – the invitation to which was the purpose of his visit – the only other guests will be Mr and Mrs Murray Posh and Miss Posh – whose existence our son has today mentioned for the first time?

JULY 4. To eight o'clock dinner at Lupin's rooms, which are very lavish; as was the food; and the wine – champagne all through the meal – and the clothes; and the jewellery (Mrs Posh told me that her necklace had cost £300!). He might have informed us that it was to be a full-dress affair; I felt quite dowdy in the dress which I bought for Mr Franching's dinner-party, even though I have only worn it once.

Lupin and Miss Lillian Posh are in love. I shall be very surprised if they are not already secretly engaged. They

I felt quite dowdy

call one another 'Lillie Girl' and 'Loopie' respectively, and she was forever pushing him, and giggling, and giving him playful slaps. It is all very like when he was engaged to Daisy Mutlar – Mrs Posh as she now is. Miss Posh is much nearer Lupin's age than Daisy, I am happy to say; I cannot say she is pretty – indeed she is plain – but she has done as much as she can to rectify the deficiencies in nature's endeavours, particularly in her hair and round the eyes. She is very tall – Lupin seems to have a *penchant* for tall women – but without the big bones and general beefiness that are so marked a feature of Mrs Posh's appearance. *She* will certainly not look ridiculous in her bridal gown.

I do *not* approve of women smoking – I blame Mr Posh for that, since he was the one who offered round Turkish cigarettes, from a gold case – and I do *not* relish being addressed as 'dear' by a chit of a girl. I believe that is how bar-maids address one another. At least Miss Posh did not express any political views, as I have heard that 'fast' young women do these days. Withal, I expect that she will improve, as has her sister-in-law – although Mrs Posh still cannot sing, as was confirmed by the dozen or so ballads she gave us! Miss Posh neither played nor sang, and so I was unable to form any opinion of her musical abilities, if any (she has the demeanour of one who might very well be proficient at the banjo).

Mr Murray Posh, who was kind enough to send us home in his carriage, was very complimentary about Lupin. He predicted (with 'Lina'!) that Lupin would go far, and become a rich man. He most certainly will if he marries Miss Posh, for Lupin told his father privately that her brother has settled £10,000 on her!

The evening held yet more in store. Arriving back at Brickfield Terrace at well past eleven, we found a cabman waiting for Charlie, with a note bidding him to the Victoria Hotel without delay, at whatever hour, to confer with Mr Hardfur Huttle, on a matter of business; and so off he went.

He came staggering in at two o'clock, having had goodness knows what to drink on top of all the champagne he was swilling down at Lupin's, and babbling about some friend of Mr Huttle's being able to put a large amount of business in Mr Perkupp's way, which would compensate him for the loss of Mr Crowbillon. I cannot understand all this business talk even at the best of times; and particularly not at that unearthly hour. I made Charlie drink a pint of warm water before going to sleep, to help his liver in the morning.

One of the happiest days of Charlie's life.

CHAPTER THE LAST

JULY 10. Tonight, whilst Charlie was writing a long letter to Lupin, proffering some very silly advice on what he imagines to be his son's improper attention to Mrs Posh (he cannot be persuaded that Lupin's interest lies elsewhere in that family!), I wrote a line to Mr Oswald Tipper, asking him to be so good as to call upon my husband, to lay before him the plan which we have discussed. I shall post the letter tomorrow morning, so that the die will be cast; and tomorrow evening, without fail, I shall sit down calmly with Charlie and inform him of what is in store. I will not tell him yet that my mind is positively made up to remove to Stonequarry Terrace – although it is – but only that he must come with me to Peckham and judge for himself, having heard Mr Tipper out as to how the expenses for the two properties compare; and then he must decide for us both, as to whether we are to remove or no. Should he decide in the negative I shall introduce rats into this house.

It is thanks to the directors and servants of the Great Northern Railway that my mind is made up, and my resolve so stern. This day, at four o'clock, it being a blazing hot afternoon, and Charlie being invited over to Mr Cummings' (for a change!) to inspect his considerable accumulation of back numbers of the *Bicycle News*, I instructed Sarah (my maid) to take the card-table and one of the dining chairs out into the garden, where I proposed to take my tea. The preparations made, I had arranged my parasol just so, and poured my tea, and cut myself a thin slice of economical currant cake, when,

'What price Cremorne Gardens!'

with a horrible clank, the semaphore signal beyond our garden wall was yanked by wires into the 'stop' position. A few moments later, a Sunday excursion train steamed into view, and with a hissing and a grinding of brakes and a shuddering of couplings, came to a halt in obedience of the signal. I do not know where it had been, and I do not care; but it was packed with East End hobbledehoys and their 'donahs,' who commenced to lean out of the windows, cupping their hands and shouting taunts and insults; what time the engine driver and his fireman grinned hugely. 'Garn!,' 'Oh, my!,' 'Ain't we the one!,' 'Wotcher, your lidyship!,' 'Ho, I s'y, Bertie, shell we hev arternoon tea wiv 'er nibs?,' and 'What price Cremorne Gardens!' were only some of the cries that assailed my ears as I hurried into the house: I will not set down the coarser expressions that were flung by the mob. As I shut the back door, there was a dull thud as something struck it – when the train had gone, I found an apple core lying on the path.

For a full five minutes the jeering continued, whilst I cowered behind the door; and then, thankfully, I heard the clank of the semaphore signal again, and the train steamed away, to resounding cheers from its uncouth passengers.

Charlie, when I gave him an account of my ordeal, took the view that I was exaggerating. He will not find a rat in his night-shirt an exaggeration.

JULY 11. Posted my letter to Mr Oswald Tipper straight after breakfast; and spent the morning walking about Holloway, rehearsing what I should say to Charlie this evening.

Upon my return home, there was a telegram waiting – a long one, of over twenty words. I was astonished to see that it was from Charlie. It informed me that in consideration of a service that he had done for the firm – the business with Mr Hardfur Huttle's friend, as it turns out – Mr Perkupp is to purchase the freehold of our house, and present it to him absolutely, as a gift.

Thus I am doomed to live out my days in Brickfield Terrace. I wrote at once to Mr Tipper, countermanding my earlier letter; and also to the Misses Tipper, regretting my inability to assist them in their aspiration to quit Peckham. I sent Sarah (my maid) off to catch the post, and thereupon sat down and wept. It was a brilliantly sunny day, and the sunbeams streaming in through the parlour window caught every speck of cinder dust from the railway. I was still weeping when Charlie arrived home early. He thought they were tears of joy; and so bemused and full of our 'good fortune' was he, that joyful my tears soon were. Dear, good Charlie! He is right –

we *have* been happy in this house, or as happy as any couple has a right to be: and we shall continue to be as happy as we are able. I shall make the best of this misfortune, as I have made the best of all the other set-backs that have come my way, and make 'The Laurels' as pretty a little home as it can be.

Charlie told me that he had also sent telegrams to Mr Gowing and Mr Cummings, inviting them to a celebratory supper, and that he proposed to send Sarah out for two bottles of 'Jackson Frères' champagne. I said: 'What a pity, on such a hot day, that it will not be chilled – it never is. If only we had a "Wenham Lake" ice safe . . .'

Charlie said: 'Carrie, my love, I will call in at Merryweather's tomorrow, and buy one, cash down, with what in our former circumstances would have been the next quarter's rent!'

The last post brought Charlie a reply to the letter that he sent off to Lupin last evening. He read it in silence, and then said: 'Hulloh! Here's one more reason for us to celebrate. Lupin writes that I have "got hold of the wrong end of the stick." He is engaged to be married to "Lillie Girl," and the wedding is to be next month!'

I said: 'I know, dear.'

I said 'I know, dear.'

234

Coming From Behind
Howard Jacobson

'A literary comedy which cuts through and beyond the Portnoy
school of self-absorbed Jewish fiction, the English University
Novel and the best of Tom Sharpe'
THE TIMES

Sefton Goldberg: mid-thirties, English teacher at Wrottesley
Poly in the West Midlands; small, sweaty, lustful, defiantly
unenamoured of beer, nature and organised games; gnawingly
aware of being an urban Jew islanded in a sea of country-
loving Anglo-Saxons. Obsessed by failure – morbidly, in his
own case, gloatingly, in that of his contemporaries – so much
so that he plans to write a bestseller on the subject. In the
meantime he is uncomfortably aware of advancing years and
atrophying achievement: and no amount of lofty
rationalisation can disguise the triumph of friends and
colleagues, not only from Cambridge days but even within the
despised walls of the Poly itself, or sweeten the bitter pill of
another's success . . .

Coming From Behind is a shrewd, articulate and consistently
hilarious successor to *Lucky Jim* and *The History Man*.

'Very funny, clever and engaging'
TIMES LITERARY SUPPLEMENT

'A sort of Jewish version of *Lucky Jim* updated for the
eighties, witty, observant, clever, a first-rate entertainment and
something more besides'
ROBERT NYE, THE GUARDIAN

0 552 99063 9   £2.95

BLACK SWAN

The Doctor's Wife
Brian Moore

'One of the outstanding works of fiction of the year'
PETER TINNISWOOD, THE TIMES

Sheila Redden is on her way from war-torn Belfast to the south
of France where her husband Kevin will join her in a few days
to relive their honeymoon of fifteen years ago. But Sheila had
not reckoned on meeting Tom Lowry and finding her life
transformed. THE DOCTOR'S WIFE is a brilliant portrait of
a woman who is suddenly confronted by the devastating power
of passionate, erotic love.

'Nightmare images of tanks cruising down empty night streets,
feverish erotic couplings with a stranger in foreign hotels; a
married woman with one son from a provincial backwater
breaking out on a trip abroad; a concerned sibling observing a
rebellious young sister; the palpable absence of God in the
central characters' lives and the notion that art and sex might
replace Him . . . the principal ingredients of Brian Moore's
fine new novel . . . a splendidly bracing experience'
NEW STATESMAN

'The erotic force of the love scenes is considerable'
THE GUARDIAN

'The most alluringly complex adulteress to come along in print
for some time'
TIME MAGAZINE

'It is uncanny; no male writer, I swear (and precious few
females), knows so much about women'
JANICE ELLIOTT, SUNDAY TELEGRAPH

0 552 99109 0   £2.50

BLACK SWAN

The Proprietor
Ann Schlee

'Rare and strange . . . rich in detail and steeped in the author's sense of the period and place about which she writes, it establishes Ann Schlee as one of the best new novelists we have'
SUSAN HILL

The islands lay low and dark in the sea that had claimed the lives of Adela Traherne's parents. Known to the islanders as the Island Child, her life became inextricably linked with Augustus Walmer, the Proprietor, in the summer of 1840 when a group of his friends came to see how he was restoring the economy and well-being of his people and the untamed beauty of the islands he owned. None of the people who came together in that summer was ever to forget what happened then, none of them was ever to break free from the island's grip, and the destinies of Adela and Augustus seemed fated to be forever linked.

'Ambitious, imaginative . . . *The Proprietor* more than a little resembles *The French Lieutenant's Woman*, with a dash of *Jamaica Inn*, and an occasional nod in the direction of *The Waves*'
ANITA BROOKNER, HARPERS & QUEEN

'Outstanding success . . . elegant precision and feeling for period . . . attractive echoes of Charlotte Bronte and Elizabeth Bowen'
HERMIONE LEE, THE OBSERVER

0 552 99099 X   £2.95

BLACK SWAN

Young Shoulders
John Wain

'A pocket classic – pleasingly trim, elegantly got together, and with an unabashed old-fashioned wish to touch the heart'
THE OBSERVER

To 17-year-old Paul Waterford, life was beginning to seem a sour business, full of unsolved problems, unhappiness and general stress. Why did his young sister Clare have to die in an air disaster? Why is his parent's marriage so evidently close to breaking up? Tired of the world as he sees it, Paul retreats into the fantasy of an ideal republic, the magnetic centre of his fantasies. But, under the pressure of extreme experiences, a lot can change in 24 hours . . .

Young Shoulders is a beautifully written account of a young man's enforced maturing, by the author of *Hurry On Down*.

'Affecting and humane'
THE STANDARD

'Wain takes a tricky subject and treats it with such assurance of clear-eyed feeling that the reader is moved to tears by his plain prose . . . a small masterpiece'
THE GUARDIAN

'A book to read and recall to mind time and again for its truth and its hope'
WHITBREAD FICTION PRIZE JUDGE

0 552 99057 4   £1.95

BLACK SWAN

In The Mood
Keith Waterhouse

'Keith Waterhouse is one of the few great writers of our time'
AUBERON WAUGH

The politicians who organised the 1951 Festival of Britain
thought they were demonstrating to the world how the British
had regenerated themselves after the war. That was not how
three northern musketeers saw it. As Raymond Watmough, the
narrator of this comic, tender chronicle of their adventures
puts it:
*'Six million pounds. Four million man-hours. A million bricks.
Six thousand six hundred tons of cement. Fifteen thousand
exhibits. Two thousand two hundred and eighty five
employees. And all so that Douglas Beckett, Terry Liversedge
and Raymond Watmough could lose their virginity . . .'*

'Riotously amusing'
THE MAIL ON SUNDAY

'Funny, touching and elegantly written; it gives a lift to the
spirits'
THE GUARDIAN

'Unquestionably brilliant and hilarious'
ALAN COREN

0 552 99074 4   £2.95

BLACK SWAN

Jumping the Queue
Mary Wesley

'A virtuoso performance of guileful plotting, deft
characterization and malicious wit'
THE TIMES

Matilda Poliport, recently widowed, has decided to End It All.
But her meticulously planned bid for graceful oblivion is
foiled, and when later she foils the suicide attempt of another
lost soul – Hugh Warner, on the run from the police – life
begins again for both.

But life also begins to throw up nasty secrets and awkward
questions: just what was Matilda's husband Tom doing in
Paris? How is the soon-to-be-knighted John (or Piers as he
likes to be called) involved? Was Louise more than just a lovely
daughter? And why did Hugh choose Matilda as his saviour?

Jumping the Queue is a brilliantly written first novel brimming
over with confidence and black humour, reminiscent of Muriel
Spark at her magnificent best.

'Great verve and inventiveness . . . (Matilda is) a convincing
original'
TIMES LITERARY SUPPLEMENT

0 552 99082 5   £1.95

BLACK SWAN